TO HOLD RESPONSIBLE

A LAKE DISTRICT THRILLER

DI SAM COBBS
BOOK TEN

M A COMLEY

Copyright © 2023 by M A Comley

All rights reserved.

No part of this book may be reproduced in any form or by any electronic or mechanical means, including information storage and retrieval systems, without written permission from the author, except for the use of brief quotations in a book review.

Thank you once again to Clive Rowlandson for allowing me to use one of his stunning photos for the cover.

ALSO BY M A COMLEY

Blind Justice (Novella)
Cruel Justice (Book #1)
Mortal Justice (Novella)
Impeding Justice (Book #2)
Final Justice (Book #3)
Foul Justice (Book #4)
Guaranteed Justice (Book #5)
Ultimate Justice (Book #6)
Virtual Justice (Book #7)
Hostile Justice (Book #8)
Tortured Justice (Book #9)
Rough Justice (Book #10)
Dubious Justice (Book #11)
Calculated Justice (Book #12)
Twisted Justice (Book #13)
Justice at Christmas (Short Story)
Prime Justice (Book #14)
Heroic Justice (Book #15)
Shameful Justice (Book #16)
Immoral Justice (Book #17)
Toxic Justice (Book #18)
Overdue Justice (Book #19)
Unfair Justice (a 10,000 word short story)
Irrational Justice (a 10,000 word short story)

Seeking Justice (a 15,000 word novella)
Caring For Justice (a 24,000 word novella)
Savage Justice (a 17,000 word novella)
Justice at Christmas #2 (a 15,000 word novella)
Gone in Seconds (Justice Again series #1)
Ultimate Dilemma (Justice Again series #2)
Shot of Silence (Justice Again series #3)
Taste of Fury (Justice Again series #4)
Crying Shame (Justice Again series #5)
See No Evil (Justice Again #6)
To Die For (DI Sam Cobbs #1)
To Silence Them (DI Sam Cobbs #2)
To Make Them Pay (DI Sam Cobbs #3)
To Prove Fatal (DI Sam Cobbs #4)
To Condemn Them (DI Sam Cobbs #5)
To Punish Them (DI Sam Cobbs #6)
To Entice Them (DI Sam Cobbs #7)
To Control Them (DI Sam Cobbs #8)
To Endanger Lives (DI Sam Cobbs #9)
To Hold Responsible (DI Sam Cobbs #10)
To Catch a Killer (DI Sam Cobbs #11)
Forever Watching You (DI Miranda Carr thriller)
Wrong Place (DI Sally Parker thriller #1)
No Hiding Place (DI Sally Parker thriller #2)
Cold Case (DI Sally Parker thriller#3)
Deadly Encounter (DI Sally Parker thriller #4)
Lost Innocence (DI Sally Parker thriller #5)
Goodbye My Precious Child (DI Sally Parker #6)

The Missing Wife (DI Sally Parker #7)
Truth or Dare (DI Sally Parker #8)
Where Did She Go? (DI Sally Parker #9)
Sinner (DI Sally Parker #10)
Web of Deceit (DI Sally Parker Novella)
The Missing Children (DI Kayli Bright #1)
Killer On The Run (DI Kayli Bright #2)
Hidden Agenda (DI Kayli Bright #3)
Murderous Betrayal (Kayli Bright #4)
Dying Breath (Kayli Bright #5)
Taken (DI Kayli Bright #6)
The Hostage Takers (DI Kayli Bright Novella)
No Right to Kill (DI Sara Ramsey #1)
Killer Blow (DI Sara Ramsey #2)
The Dead Can't Speak (DI Sara Ramsey #3)
Deluded (DI Sara Ramsey #4)
The Murder Pact (DI Sara Ramsey #5)
Twisted Revenge (DI Sara Ramsey #6)
The Lies She Told (DI Sara Ramsey #7)
For The Love Of… (DI Sara Ramsey #8)
Run for Your Life (DI Sara Ramsey #9)
Cold Mercy (DI Sara Ramsey #10)
Sign of Evil (DI Sara Ramsey #11)
Indefensible (DI Sara Ramsey #12)
Locked Away (DI Sara Ramsey #13)
I Can See You (DI Sara Ramsey #14)
The Kill List (DI Sara Ramsey #15)
Crossing The Line (DI Sara Ramsey #16)

Time to Kill (DI Sara Ramsey #17)
Deadly Passion (DI Sara Ramsey #18)
Son Of The Dead (DI Sara Ramsey #19)
Evil Intent (DI Sara Ramsey #20)
The Games People Play (DI Sara Ramsey #21)
I Know The Truth (A Psychological thriller)
She's Gone (A psychological thriller)
Shattered Lives (A psychological thriller)
Evil In Disguise – a novel based on True events
Deadly Act (Hero series novella)
Torn Apart (Hero series #1)
End Result (Hero series #2)
In Plain Sight (Hero Series #3)
Double Jeopardy (Hero Series #4)
Criminal Actions (Hero Series #5)
Regrets Mean Nothing (Hero series #6)
Prowlers (Di Hero Series #7)
Sole Intention (Intention series #1)
Grave Intention (Intention series #2)
Devious Intention (Intention #3)
Cozy mysteries
Murder at the Wedding
Murder at the Hotel
Murder by the Sea
Death on the Coast
Death By Association
Merry Widow (A Lorne Simpkins short story)
It's A Dog's Life (A Lorne Simpkins short story)

A Time To Heal (A Sweet Romance)

A Time For Change (A Sweet Romance)

High Spirits

The Temptation series (Romantic Suspense/New Adult Novellas)

Past Temptation

Lost Temptation

Clever Deception (co-written by Linda S Prather)

Tragic Deception (co-written by Linda S Prather)

Sinful Deception (co-written by Linda S Prather)

ACKNOWLEDGMENTS

Special thanks as always go to @studioenp for their superb cover design expertise.

My heartfelt thanks go to my wonderful editor Emmy, and my proofreaders Joseph and Barbara for spotting all the lingering nits.

Thank you also to my amazing ARC Group who help to keep me sane during this process.

RIP Mum, you've taken a huge part of my heart with you. Until we meet again.

To Mary, gone, but never forgotten. I hope you found the peace you were searching for my dear friend. I miss you each and every day.

PROLOGUE

"This is nice," Fiona said. She hugged John and glanced up at him.

He smiled down at her. It had been a hectic week, and this was the perfect end of a frantic day, sitting in their home cinema, watching a film they'd been desperate to see for a while together, *Maverick*.

Their daughter, Chrissie, who was fifteen going on thirty, sat in one of the special viewing chairs a few seats down from him, giving the movie her full attention for a change, rather than having her mobile glued to her hands.

Next to her was Adam; he had just turned thirteen. This was a late birthday treat for him, the film choice had been his. They tried to let everyone choose a film in rotation, anything for an easy life, to help make movie nights more enjoyable with teens around.

The movie had only been on five minutes, and John was engrossed already. He had loved *Top Gun*, the original, and was dying to see Maverick's new adventure and where it would lead him this time around. He'd always been a huge admirer of Tom Cruise, particularly the *Mission Impossible* movies. He couldn't wait for the new one to come out as Cruise and the film crew had been spotted down the road from them, filming around Buttermere only last year. Mind you, who could blame them? It was a stunning, and often dramatic place to visit, let alone shoot a Hollywood movie.

During a lull in the action, his attention was drawn to a noise in the kitchen. John glanced at his wife; she'd heard it, too. "You stay here, I'll go. It's probably the cat or one of the cartons from the takeaway crackling as it cools down."

"Shall we put the film on pause?"

John shook his head. He himself hated viewing a film when it was stopped and started several times. It took the enjoyment out of it. "No, you carry on, it's loud enough for me to hear what's going on from out there anyway. I'll be back in a second."

Fiona smiled and grabbed another handful of popcorn from the tub sitting on the floor beside them.

"Dad, watch it, you nearly crushed my foot," Adam complained as John inched past him with one eye still on the screen.

"Sorry, I wasn't watching where I was going."

"Doh, that much is evident," Adam grumbled.

John shrugged and left the room. He closed the door behind him and began the search to find out where the strange noise had come from. He briefly poked his head into the lounge and then the dining room. Nope, nothing in either room. That just left the downstairs toilet and the kitchen to check. He opened the door to the loo, nothing in there either, and then finally moved on to the kitchen. The metal takeaway dishes were still on the worktop, along with the paper bags they'd come in. John had ordered the delivery himself, and Fiona had dished up once it had arrived. It was his job to tidy up, but he hadn't got around to doing it as the kids, and Fiona, were all eager to settle down to the film. It hadn't taken much to persuade him to leave the mess until after the film had finished. Talking of which, he was keen to get back to it and scanned the kitchen a second time. Everything still looked in place to him. His gaze rose to the back door which he spotted was ajar several inches. Now that was definitely out of place. Neither he nor his wife ever left it open, not even in the summer, or maybe they did during the day, however, it was never an option in the evening, not when they were elsewhere in the house, or as in tonight's case, they were distracted watching a movie.

John took two steps closer. A few muddy footprints marred the shiny travertine tiles closest to the back door. He paused, sensing someone was behind him. Too scared to turn and face the intruder, he tried to get away, but a transparent plastic bag was pulled over his head and tightened around his neck. He sucked in, and the bag followed his breath into his mouth, making him gag.

He sank to his knees, the intruder's grip never faltering. He stared up at the masked person whom he perceived to be a man, given the strength applied to keep him restrained. The man worked quickly, tying the bag in place. John's eyes widened as he struggled for breath, the panic rising within. His organs took it in turns to burn, adding to his terrifying ordeal. The person let him go and swiftly grabbed a metal bar leaning against the end of the kitchen island which John had neglected to see. The intruder's intention was perfectly clear when he slapped the bar up and down in the palm of his right hand.

John shielded his face with his arm and begged, or tried to, given the restrictions over his airways, "Please, why are you doing this? Tell me what you want and I will give it to you."

The person growled and smashed the bar against John's legs, not once, but twice. The force was that intense, the pain scorched his lungs and hampered his breathing further. It didn't take John long to realise that the blow had smashed a couple of bones. "No, don't do this. Tell me what you want." He was desperate to keep this madman away from his family. If that meant taking the brunt of the force, then so be it despite his erratic breathing.

The intruder took another couple of steps towards him. The bar rose above his head once more and dropped with an almighty thud, doing untold damage to John's knees this time. He cried out, but the intruder slapped a hand over his mouth, silencing him.

"Please tell me what you want. Why are you doing this?" he asked through clenched teeth, fighting the urge to scream out as the pain intensified in his knees. He'd never known such crippling agony, not even when he'd broken his leg on a skiing trip several years before. His breathing was becoming more and more laboured.

The man shuffled closer, leaned in and whispered, "I want what you took from me. This is my revenge. You and your family will suffer at my hands tonight. There will be no escaping what I have planned for you, all of you, so do not try to prevent it. Not that you're in a position to do that."

The bar swung high above the intruder's head and came swinging down again, striking John's knees a second time. The crunching sound took John's breath away. His mind reeled, his urge to warn his family multiplying with every suffocating breath he took. If he succeeded in his mission, would they try and run? Would they even hear his suppressed attempt above the noise of the film?

However, the person looming over him had other ideas. The bag was pulled tighter, cutting off his airway completely. His grappling at the intruder's arms and muffled cries for help were met with a defiant shake of the man's head.

His head dropped lower, to within inches of John's, and

he sneered, "You have my word that your loved ones will suffer before they meet their maker. It will be my pleasure to take each of their lives, and yours as well."

He lifted the bar above John's head, and it came crashing down, the target this time not his legs but his skull, the blow successfully knocking John out cold.

CHAPTER 1

Bob thrust his head around the door to Sam's office, catching her daydreaming about the glorious weekend away she had spent with Rhys, Sonny and Casper, the pup with rubber legs who was rapidly growing daily.

"Sorry, did you want something, Bob?"

"I was wondering if you were busy. The last thing I'd want to do is disturb you from getting on with your onerous chores."

Sam poked her tongue out and gave him the finger. "Up yours. What's up?"

"We've had a call. Suspected break-in that has resulted in a family being murdered."

Sam wheeled her chair back and rose to her feet. "What the fuck? Where?"

"On the outskirts of Workington, on that posh new estate out at Stainburn."

"What are we waiting for? We'd better get our skates on and get over there, tout de suite."

"Search me. Hey, don't shoot the messenger, it wasn't me

who was daydreaming about their romantic interlude while they should have been striving to deplete their paperwork."

Sam's cheeks heated up, and she elbowed him in the ribs. They were halfway down the stairs when Sam remembered she hadn't brought her jacket and ID with her.

"Damn, I'll be right back." She returned to the incident room and rolled her eyes. "He's never going to let me live this one down," she said to no one in particular. After retrieving her jacket and warrant card, she retraced her steps and asked the team, "You're aware of what's happened, I take it? Get the ball rolling with the usual while we're out. I'll update you as and when."

"Yes, boss," her colleagues responded in unison.

It wasn't until she'd caught up with Bob that she wondered how much the team had been told about the incident. *Crap, I really need to concentrate more when I'm at work and stop bloody daydreaming. I've slipped up but I'm not about to admit it to Bob. He'd have a field day if I did.*

TEN MINUTES LATER, they arrived at the exclusive estate consisting of a dozen or so bespoke homes. The journey had been conducted in relative silence. Bob had divulged the mere basics of what to expect upon their arrival. Sam drew the car to a halt alongside the pathologist's van. A SOCO vehicle was at the site, too. Behind the cordon, several onlookers strained their necks to see the events unfold.

"I expected better from a community like this," Sam complained.

"It's a natural response. I don't think it matters how much money you have in the bank."

Sam chortled. "Thanks for the clarification, Bob. I'll be sure to make a note of that for future reference."

He gave her a cheesy grin and said, "Glad to be of

assistance. You know me, always keen to point out the obvious."

"Ain't that the frigging truth?" Sam muttered.

"Are you two at it again?" a stern voice said from behind, startling Sam.

"Ah, Mr Markham, there you are. And how are we today?"

"I don't know about you, but I'm pretty pissed off, constipated, and I haven't eaten in hours, but hey-ho, as you know, that tends to go with the territory."

Sam suppressed the giggle tickling her throat. "All except the constipation. Did you have to share that particular snippet of personal information with me?"

"Sharing is caring as they say. If I'm suffering then I feel ten times better knowing that those around me are aware that I'm like a bear with a sore backside, literally."

Sam winced. "Duly noted. What have we got here?"

"You'd better get suited up. I'll sort out some masks for you as well. It ain't pretty, but you're going to need to assess the scene with your own eyes rather than me tell you what I think went on in there."

"Sounds ominous." Sam groaned internally. "Have you got any supplies we can pinch?"

"Jesus, woman, you never cease to amaze me. You're the only inspector I know who has the audacity to try and get blood out of a stone. We're dealing with major cutbacks as well as you, you know. All that shit with the pandemic, having to change suits and PPE every ten minutes or so, is coming back and biting the department in the arse right now. Ouch, did I have to mention that sodding area of my anatomy again? My fault, as if I'm not suffering enough."

"All right, it was a simple question, there's no need to bite my head off. I'll see what I've got tucked away in the back of my car."

"Do me a favour! You know I'll supply what you need, but it comes with a warning: you need to up the amount you carry in your vehicle. We've had instructions not to share unnecessarily at a crime scene. So that means, gone are the days I hand out suits like sodding Smarties, got that?"

Sam mock saluted. "Received, loud and clear, and will be enforced promptly, I promise."

"Good. Now let's crack on, shall we? Time is money and all that nonsense."

He rummaged in the back of the van and collected two paper suits that he aimed at Bob, who passed one to Sam. After they had togged up, Des dipped back into the van and withdrew two gas masks, gloves and shoe covers, which he also handed to Bob.

Sam frowned. "Are these necessary?"

Des stared at her. "Do you really need to ask that question?"

"Shit. We'd better get in there and find out for ourselves."

"As I suggested, over five minutes ago," Des bit back, glancing at his watch. He marched through the front door of the detached house.

"Consider yourself told," Bob said and pulled his mask into place.

"Yep. Happy days. So glad I love my chosen career. If I didn't, I fear I would have jacked it in a long time ago, rather than having to deal with that obnoxious man. I can understand why his assistant told him to stick his job up his jacksy."

"He's not that bad. The trouble with you is, you allow him to wind you up all the time, and don't get me started on his assistant. You know as well as I do she wasn't cut out for this job."

"You're right, I do. I'll tell you this, though, my working

life is never dull when I have two strong-willed men to deal with on a daily basis."

Bob stopped mid-stride and faced her. "Er... and who's the other one?"

Sam stared at him and cocked an eyebrow. "A good detective should be able to work things out for himself, without the need of further hints."

"Bloody charming, that is. Right, no more Mr Nice Guy from me, I won't be bloody holding back in the future."

"Good, I'll look forward to you adding some valuable insight to this case in the near future then."

Sam laughed and turned her back on him. He mumbled something indecipherable from behind the mask.

"I heard that," she said. Even though she hadn't caught what he'd muttered, she recognised his tone of insolence, despite his voice being inhibited by the equipment.

She entered the large entrance hall of the house. The stark white walls weren't really to her taste, they made the area feel cold, and Sam shuddered a little. Although, maybe that was more to do with what lay ahead of her than her surroundings. She strolled past the large sweeping oak staircase and followed the trail of bags and equipment lying outside a room off to the right.

After checking her mask was secured and sitting in the appropriate position, she peered around the corner and gasped.

"Come in, don't be shy," Des beckoned her. He stood close to the body of a woman in her fifties. She was blonde and had a petite frame.

Sam's eyes misted. "Mother and two children, I'm guessing."

"Holy shit!" Bob said, louder than he'd probably intended behind her.

"Precisely. What a waste," Des agreed. "Eliminated while they were enjoying a movie."

"Why the need for the masks?" Sam scanned the room. It was fairly large, set out with six comfy seats. *Does that mean there are six members of this family, or are the other three chairs for guests?*

"Feel free to take it off," Des said, interrupting her thoughts. "If you think you can handle the smell."

"Smell? Decaying flesh?" Sam asked, perplexed.

The three bodies all appeared to be relatively intact, no sign of decomposition, not to her untrained eye.

"Gas. They were *gassed*, Inspector."

"Shit! What the fuck? Do we know how?"

Des pointed at a canister lying on the floor. "It's crude, but effective nonetheless."

"How the fuck does someone get hold of something like that in this country?" Sam took two paces towards the canister for a closer look.

"You'll be surprised what you can buy off the internet these days," Bob replied.

"I agree," Des said. "We'll need to get it analysed back at the lab, see what it consisted of and see where that leads us."

"Are you suggesting that something was bought and then possibly tampered with, making it more lethal?"

"Who knows? Like I said, we'll need to leave it to the lab, see what they can decipher."

"Either way, this has murder written all over it. Bringing something like that to a scene is premeditated, right?"

Des nodded his agreement. "There's something else you should know."

Sam inclined her head, her gaze shifting back to the three victims sitting in the comfy seats. "Which is?"

"The missing piece to this puzzle," Des said cryptically.

"And that is? God, Des, spit it out, will you?"

"The husband."

"What about him? Are you telling me he did this? How do you know? Have you found a note or something? You're going to have to give me more than that, Des."

"When I get the chance to get a word in, I will. He was found in the kitchen and has since been taken to hospital, suffering from life-threatening injuries."

"Shit! Was he to blame for their deaths, is that what you're telling me?"

Des shook his head and shrugged. "I don't think so. I arrived as the ambulance was taking him away. The injuries he sustained... well, in my professional opinion, there is no way he could have done that to himself."

"So someone injured him and then killed his family, or was it the other way round, killed his family and he possibly walked in and got clobbered before the killer left the scene?"

"That, my dear inspector, is a question you'll need to find the answer to yourself."

"Was the husband conscious?"

"No. We found a plastic bag beside him, I'm presuming the perpetrator tied it around his head at one time because it was scrunched up at the bottom as if it had been tied."

The killer must have wanted him to survive. Why? "Who reported the crime, if he was unconscious? Is there another member of the family that we're missing here?"

"No, the cleaner reported the crime and called for an ambulance to attend."

Sam didn't recall seeing anyone outside, not on this side of the cordon anyway. "Where are they?"

"She lives in the next road, on the smaller estate." He withdrew a card and handed it to her. "I wrote her name and address on the back."

"Thanks. I'll nip and see her soon."

"Be gentle with her, she's pretty shaken up. I had to give

her husband a call to come and collect her because her legs refused to work properly."

"Poor woman. Of course I'll go easy on her. Could she tell you anything else?"

"Again, you know me. I detest dealing with members of the public at a scene. It's bad enough when they show up to view their loved ones after I've carried out a PM. I only just managed to get her address out of her, amidst the tears and snot on show."

Sam tutted. "You're an uncaring bastard at times, Des Markham."

"Yep, I'm not about to deny that charge either, although I have to say my wife and daughter will disagree with you, occasionally."

"Very occasionally," Sam batted back snarkily.

"Get you, little Miss Perfect with your squeaky-clean lifestyle, new beau and…"

She raised a hand to prevent the conversation sinking to a new low. "Would it be all right if we got back to business now? This is a very serious crime scene we're attending, in case you hadn't noticed."

"Oh, I noticed all right, the instant I arrived."

"Have your guys checked upstairs?"

"They carried out a brief search, but there are no further members of the family up there."

"Would it be okay if I had a look for myself?"

"By all means. You know the drill, no touching anything without your gloves on."

Sam rolled her eyes but chose to ignore his comment rather than get into another time-wasting confrontation with him. She got the feeling that Des Markham was under pressure, regretting the fact that his assistant had dumped him and walked away from the job she had loved so much because of the way he had treated her in the past. Sam had seen it with her own eyes, even pulled Des up on it as recently as a few months before, but his willingness to ignore what was in front of him still pissed her off.

Your loss, matey. Yes, you're an exceptional pathologist, there's no denying that, however, as far as your caring human nature is concerned... well, that remains clearly disguised.

"I take it photos have been taken of every room?"

"You presume right," Des replied stiffly.

Bob followed Sam out of the room and tutted once they removed their masks in the hallway. "Why do you allow him to do that?"

"Keep your gloves on. What?" Sam demanded, perplexed.

"Wind you up like that?"

Sam heaved out a breath. "Let's face it, all Markham has to do is open his mouth and he winds me up."

"You two need your heads knocked together. He's superb at his job, Sam, you have to admit that."

"I'm not saying he isn't. I've never been critical about his work, but his attitude and his inability to speak to colleagues properly suck, you have to admit that."

"I do. This is about that assistant of his, or should I say his former assistant, isn't it?"

"What if it is? Kathryn had a heart of gold, and he shot her down in flames most days. Made her question her own self-worth and drove her out of the business."

"Let's be fair, we all know what he's like. If she couldn't handle the way he spoke to her then she should have put in a complaint with the Home Office, not that she would have got very far."

"Precisely, what would have been the point? Anyway, Kathryn's moved on to pastures new and has job satisfaction at the end of the day. That means the be all and end all to some people."

"Yeah, but I bet her salary sucks. Have you seen her since she left?"

"Yes, Rhys and I visited the restaurant where she's now working and, to be honest, she seemed far more smiley and relaxed. I had a quiet word with her on the night, and she told me her boss appreciated her which went a long way towards her job satisfaction."

"That's not what I said. I was talking about her wages."

"She said she makes enough to pay her bills, and the tips she earns allows her to treat herself now and again."

"Good for her. But seriously, you women need to stop expecting us men to give you an easy time. After all, you've been fighting for equality for decades now."

Sam's eyes widened, and her anger bubbled within. She took a step closer to him and prodded him in the chest as she spoke through gritted teeth, "This isn't about equality, and you damn well know it. Women have the right to be treated the same as their male counterparts in the workplace. The sooner you, and the likes of Professor Des Markham, realise that the better. Now that you've wound me up tighter than a coiled spring, shall we get on with the investigation?"

Bob stared at her finger that was still prodding at his pecs. "If you insist. Touchy subject but one that needs to be highlighted now and again, right?"

"Not if you value your role as my partner. Shall we continue, eh?"

"Wow! That's a great way to start the day, with a threat from your boss."

"You forgot to add your *female* boss," Sam added and made her way up the sweeping staircase.

"There you go again… I repeat, you women demand equality when it suits you, but when it comes to getting the top off a bottle or something as equally mundane, you always resort to fluttering your eyelashes at us, hoping we'll step in and get the job done."

Sam did her best to suppress the laugh threatening to erupt and carried on up the stairs. At the top, she faked tripping up the final step just to see what his reaction would be. He didn't let her down, he came to her assistance swiftly.

"Hey, are you okay?"

She fluttered her eyelashes and placed a hand over her chest. "My hero. You saved me. I knew you would come to my aid, you always do."

"Jesus… you're sick. I can't believe I fell for that one, again."

She swiped his arm and released the laugh she'd been holding in. "Gullible, that's what you are. Mission accomplished. Moving on."

"I wish you would," he grumbled.

They travelled the length of the hallway. Sam poked her head around every door they approached, searching for the main bedroom which ended up being the final room they encountered.

"Here we are. Let's see what we can find, if anything, in here."

The first thing Sam noticed was the décor. It was subtle, in a style that would appeal to both genders. Again, the walls were mostly white, however, there was a panel of rich blue behind the large buttoned fabric headboard. The patch of colour was enhanced by a wooden rail that had been painted in a different shade of blue, a much lighter colour. On either side of the king-sized bed were mirrored bedside tables and, against the wall under the window, was a matching dressing table which sparkled in the rays of the sun filtering through the window. A crystal chandelier hung from the ceiling, directly above the bed.

Sam took a few steps closer to the dressing table. She

picked up the family photo of whom she presumed to be the mother, father and their two children. She recognised the woman and the kids as those who had perished in the home cinema.

Sam shook her head. "Des is right about one thing."

Bob came to stand beside her, his paper suit rustling as he moved. "What's that?"

"It's a damn waste. Three young lives, gone, just like that. The question is, why? Why would someone break into their home, kill the wife and two kids and leave the husband alive?"

"Maybe they thought the husband was lying dead in the kitchen and then they killed the rest of the family and left."

"Without checking he was dead? What if it was intentional?"

"Leaving him alive to deal with the consequences?"

"Possibly. We won't know that until we have a chat with him, whenever that might be, the state he's in. Let's face it, we've got no idea what kind of injuries he has suffered."

Bob sighed. "Life-threatening only means one thing in my opinion; he's on the brink of hanging on to life."

"Yep, that much I figured out for myself, partner. At least we now know that the family only consisted of the adults and two kids."

"Unless we come across another photo to dismiss that theory. Maybe that's their immediate family, perhaps they've got other kids off at university or older, who have left home."

"Point taken. We need to find out what the family dynamics are, that needs to be our first step."

"Really?"

"Why are you challenging me?"

"I'm not. I would have thought speaking with the witness would be our first port of call."

"Of course, it still remains our priority. All I was saying

was... oh, it doesn't matter, I shouldn't need to explain how an investigation works to a man of your intelligence."

Bob tutted and shook his head. "I'd give up, if I were you."

"Yep, I think you're right. Let's see if we can find any paperwork lying around. I'll try the wardrobe. Why don't you search the bedside cabinets?"

They parted and set off in different directions. Sam opened the mirrored wardrobe doors. Her eye was immediately drawn to the colour-ordered clothes on the rails. It was like staring at a rainbow.

"Amazing," she whispered.

"Did you say something?" Bob shouted.

"No, you probably wouldn't get it anyway."

"Says you," her partner grumbled in response.

"Get on with the search and stop whingeing." She glanced up at the two shelves at the top of the built-in wardrobe and then peered over her shoulder in the hope of finding a chair to give her the extra height she'd need to see if there was anything of use up there.

She crossed the room to fetch the stool in front of the dressing table.

"Do you need a hand?" Bob asked.

Sam was determined to complete the task on her own. "Nope, I'm fine."

"Give me a shout if you're struggling."

"As if," she murmured in response. She stood on the heavy stool, but it neglected to give her the height she needed to view what was on the shelves. "Do you mind?" she asked.

"Wow, twice in one day I've come to your assistance. My hero status must be sky-high right now, eh?"

"Get on with it and quit trying to piss me off."

"What do you need?"

"To see if there's a box with personal paperwork hidden at the back, like there usually is."

"Not in my house there isn't. We use a personal file to store all our valuable docs."

"Me, too. Which reminds me, I haven't had a good clear-out for a while, there's bound to be stuff still in there from when Chris and I were together."

"I would have thought that would have been the first thing you did, have a clear-out, rid yourself of his memory and the memories you created together."

"Get you. All the memories I have of him revolve around the debts he left me with after he killed himself."

"You must have created some good memories, too, over the years, Sam, didn't you?"

"I suppose. I think I've chosen to blank them out. Still, there's no point in me dwelling on that now." She took a step back, for a better view. When that failed, she climbed onto the bed and bounced. "Yes, there, at the back, there's a clear box. No, to your right, go on, you're nearly there now."

Bob stood on tiptoes. The stool wobbled beneath his twelve-stone frame before he toppled to the floor.

"What did you do that for? You were almost there. It was within your grasp."

Bob stared at her for a moment or two then got to his feet and brushed himself down. "I'm fine, no damage done, but thanks for asking, boss."

She leapt off the bed and ran towards him. "I'm so sorry, Bob. Are you all right?"

"I'll survive. I ain't risking my neck on that thing again. I'll have a hunt around for a set of steps. I'll be right back."

Sam continued to search the bedside tables in his absence until he returned, a set of steps clunking against his shins when he entered the bedroom.

"Damn things. I'm going to have bruises galore now."

"And not from me, that'll be a first." Sam laughed, but her partner's expression remained serious.

"Whatever," he said finally. He placed the steps where the stool had been moments earlier and climbed up to the top rung. "I should reach it this time. Yes, here it is." He stretched onto the shelf and pulled the box from the back to the front without much effort. "It's pretty light, lighter than I expected it to be. Do you want to take it from me?"

Sam stepped towards him and held out her arms to accept the box, which Bob dropped and she caught safely.

"You're right, it is light. Doesn't bode well, does it?"

Bob shrugged. "There's no point in speculating, just open it and see."

Sam placed the box on the bed and removed the lid. She rummaged through the contents to reveal the normal paperwork: four birth certificates and one of marriage. "It confirms there were only the four of them, I believe."

Bob peeked over her shoulder. "Four birth certificates. If they had older kids, wouldn't they have taken theirs with them?"

"Possibly. Anyway, this will do us for now. We need to nip and have a word with the cleaner, she'll be thinking we've forgotten about her."

"Maybe she'll be on another job," Bob suggested.

"Nah, I can't see it. Not if she was as shaken up as Des made her out to be. I'll let SOCO know about the box when we go downstairs. Are you fit? Forget I asked that, after the fall you've just had."

"I lost my balance, no big deal. It was a tiny stool, too small to take my frame. I should have realised that before I got up there."

"But you didn't."

"Why is this my fault? You're the one who was keen to get your hands on the box, or are you forgetting that?"

"No comment. Come on, Twinkle Toes, we've got work to do."

SAM KNOCKED on the front door of the semi-detached house a couple of streets from the crime scene. A man in his late fifties to early sixties opened the front door.

"Mr Finch?"

"That's right. You must be the police, we were told to expect you."

Sam showed her ID and introduced herself and Bob to the man who then took a step back and gestured for them to join him in the hallway.

"Cynthia is in there. I have to warn you, she's a mess. Finding the family the way she did, well, it has knocked the bloody stuffing out of her. She loved that family, all of them, as if they were her own."

"I'm so sorry she had to make the gruesome discovery. Do you think she's up to speaking with us?"

"She's a strong character. She'll bounce back. I'm sure she'll be fine, once she gets started. The tears keep coming and going when she least expects them to, I wanted you to be aware of that from the get-go. Please be gentle with her. The family meant the world to her. She wasn't just their cleaner, she often looked after the kids, too, when the parents had other things on their plate, you know, meetings or just general work stuff."

"I understand. We'll conduct the interview at her pace, I promise you."

"Very well. Do either of you want a drink?"

"Two coffees, white with one sugar would be wonderful, thank you."

Mr Finch nodded and opened the door to the lounge. He stepped in and shuffled to the side, allowing Sam and Bob to join him.

"Love, this is DI Dobbs and her partner, I'm sorry, I'm not very good with names at the best of times."

Sam smiled. "No need to apologise. Hello, Mrs Finch. I'm Detective Inspector Sam Cobbs of the Cumbria Constabulary, and this is my partner, DS Bob Jones. I know you've had a severe shock today, finding the Wade family like that. Are you up to talking to us?"

"Oh, yes." Mrs Finch sniffled. "Come in and take a seat. Has Mick offered to make you a drink? He makes a great cuppa."

"I have, I'm on my way to fetch them now. Do you want another, Cyn?"

"Why not? It's not like I've got anything better to do today than to stare into the bottom of my mug. I'm sorry, I don't mean to come across as gloomy. Thanks, Mick, you're an angel."

"I know you don't mean it. I'll be back shortly."

"Do you need a hand, Mr Finch?" Sam asked.

The man seemed in a confused state, and she was worried about him.

"No, I'll be fine. You stay here and have a chat with Cyn." He shuffled out of the room and closed the door behind him.

"He's trying to convince me he's all right but he's not, far from it. He adored those kids as much as I did. We often took them on picnics at the weekend when the parents had work to do." Cynthia stopped and wiped her nose on a tissue that she withdrew from her sleeve.

"This must be hard for you. I want you to take your time. If you find the interview getting too much, let me know and we'll end it, okay?"

"Yes, thank you for being so understanding. I can't work out how or why something like this should happen to such a wonderful family."

"That's what we intend to find out, but we're going to

need your help. Any information you can give us today will prove valuable to the investigation, I assure you. So, please, don't hold back."

"I won't. I want to tell you everything, I need to. I want you to catch the person responsible for robbing that family of their lives. I know John is still alive, but you didn't see how badly injured he was when I found him. His head was caved in and his legs broken in several places." She slapped a hand over her mouth. "Who could carry out such a violent act on a person? Why? And why kill his family, Fiona, Chrissie and Adam? None of this makes any sense to me at all."

"First of all, I need to ascertain if there are any other family members in the area."

Cynthia covered her eyes with her hand and sobbed.

Sam moved closer to the woman on the sofa and flung an arm around her shoulders. "Try not to upset yourself, I know how difficult this must be for you."

"It truly is. John's mother and father…" She sniffled. "They live on the other side of Workington, out in one of the villages. Shit, should I have rung them? I didn't know what to do. I suppose it's one of those occasions when you're damned if you do and damned if you don't. I wouldn't have known what to say to them, not really."

"Don't be worried about that. The responsibility should lie with us. If you can give me their names and address, we can call there after we leave here this morning."

"Yes, it's Iris and Albert Wade; he likes to be called Bert, though. I'll have to look up their address in my notebook. I'll be right back."

Sam placed a hand on Cynthia's leg. "There's no rush, you can give it to me later, don't worry."

The door opened, and her husband entered the room with a tray and four mugs. Bob jumped to his feet to assist the man.

"Clear that table, will you, please?" Mr Finch asked.

Bob gathered the magazines and paper from the table and slid them onto the shelf below. Mr Finch placed the tray on the table and distributed the mugs.

Sam smiled and accepted two mugs, one for herself and one for Cynthia. "I'll take your wife's. How are you, Cynthia?"

The woman sniffed and wiped the tissue under her nose. "I'm all right. Better than that poor man and his family. That image... those images... will remain with me for the rest of my life. Heartbreaking and so unnecessary. How could someone do that to them? How? This is supposed to be a decent neighbourhood. Not in the same class as theirs, granted, but who could kill that beautiful family?"

Sam sipped at her much-needed cup of coffee and contemplated where to lead the conversation next. Her gaze flicked between the husband and wife, who both seemed shell-shocked by the events that had unfolded. "Have you worked for them long? Known them long?"

"It's a new house, they've only lived here about a year. I answered an ad they ran in the local paper and I got the job on the day I applied to be their cleaner. At first, I thought they only gave me the job because I lived a few streets away, but then, the longer I worked for them, the closer we became. It wasn't long before Fiona was confiding in me about all sorts. She trusted me with the kids. We used to take them out regularly, or have Chrissie and Adam round here for dinner sometimes if Fiona and John had a special engagement they had to attend. The kids were angels, well, compared to those you see hanging out on the corners in town, drinking, causing a fuss, shouting and dropping litter everywhere. Not Chrissie and Adam, they were polite, had impeccable manners. They enjoyed being with their parents and treated every adult they met with respect. Just like when we were growing up, eh, Mick?"

"Aye, that's right, love. Just like the old days, when adults had a say in the way their kids behaved. They don't seem to have that these days. Nowt a good thrashing wouldn't put right."

"Now, Mick, you know as well as I do that parents aren't allowed to hit their children these days, or should I say, show them the error of their ways," Cynthia corrected her husband, casting a wary eye in Sam's direction.

Sam winced. "I'll pretend I didn't hear that." She winked at Mick. "But yes, my father hit me on occasion, to keep me in line when I was in my teens."

"A little tearaway, were you?" Mick asked.

"I had my moments. We all seem to think we know better than our parents at that age, don't we?"

"We do, I'll give you that." Mick smiled.

"You say they started to confide in you, can you tell me what that comprised of?"

"I don't know really. Anything and everything. Fiona had a health scare at the beginning of the year. I supported her throughout her treatment. Took the children off her hands while she had chemo. I used to make them dinner and looked after them until John came home from work. It was the least I could do; she didn't want to burden John's parents. His father has heart problems, so they were conscious about not heaping any extra stress on him, fearing it would be too much for him."

"Thanks for the heads-up. We'll watch out for the signs when we break the news."

Mick shook his head. "This news is likely to finish him off."

Cynthia reached for her husband's hand. "Don't say that, love."

"Why not? It's true."

They stared at each other for a second or two, and then Cynthia shrugged.

"I suppose so. But they're going to need to be told all the same."

"Don't worry, we'll take every precaution we can whilst we tell them. Watch out for the signs et cetera," Sam responded.

"Oh, yes, I'm not saying you would go in there and just blurt it out," Cynthia replied. "But are you medically trained, is that what you're telling us?"

"No, not at all. But I have had to deal with incidents where people's health has suffered once the shock hits them."

Cynthia took a sip of her drink and said, "I don't envy you your job, not at all."

"It has its good moments, I promise you."

"Like when you bang up the person responsible for killing that family?" Mick asked.

"Exactly. Do you know what kind of careers the parents had? Or did, in Fiona's case."

"Yes, John runs some kind of export business, don't ask me what he exports. All I can tell you is that he does a lot of hours and is passionate about his work."

Bob jotted down the information in his notebook.

"And Fiona?"

"She's only just gone back to work, you know, since her illness. She runs a boutique with one of her friends in Workington. It's only a small shop, but their trade mostly comes in from online. They had to diversify during the pandemic. It was a struggle, but they managed to pull it off and were reaping the benefits towards the end of last year. But then the cancer struck and knocked the bloody stuffing out of her. That's why I pleaded with her to let me help look after the kids. She was exhausted most of the time. Not that the kids were a handful, they weren't, but every child has needs. Chrissie and Adam belonged to quite a few after-school clubs, and they had a lot of interests, like piano classes for Chrissie, and Adam enjoyed archery. His father used to go to the club often, when time permitted."

"Is that local?"

"Yes, in Workington. Mick can tell you more about that side of things than I can."

Mick shrugged, and his mouth turned down at the sides. "Oh, can I? I guess I used to watch Adam when I picked him up. I was impressed the number of times he hit the target. He encouraged me to have a go, but I was useless. You definitely need to have the knack for something like that. When I tried, I didn't even hit the outer rings. Way off the mark, I was."

Sam smiled. "And where did Chrissie have lessons for the piano, can you tell me?"

"Oh, that used to take place at the house. They have a large music room in the garden, a purpose-built one, which they had installed a few months after they moved in."

"Did Chrissie have any other hobbies of note?" Sam asked.

"Not really. Not unless you include her love of butterflies and bees. There was talk of them putting a few hives in the garden, but the garden would need to be landscaped first, to encourage the bees, that sort of thing."

"I see, and what about John and Fiona, can you tell me what sort of marriage they had? Were they happy? Any arguments lately? Anything we should be aware of?"

The couple glanced at each other again and shook their heads.

Cynthia swallowed, and tears bulged. "No, I would have to say that I've rarely seen or heard them argue. They seemed happy enough to us, didn't they, Mick?"

"One of the happiest couples around, I would say, apart from us, darling," Mick replied with a smile.

"Get away with you, even we have the odd spat now and again."

"Aye, but the making up makes it all worthwhile, doesn't it?"

Sam noticed the twinkle enter his eyes and the colour appear in Cynthia's cheeks.

Cynthia laughed. "Ignore him. He deliberately sets out to embarrass me in front of strangers, it's a hobby of his."

Mick grinned in response.

"Did either John or Fiona mention if they had any financial concerns they were dealing with?"

Cynthia paused to think. "No, nothing in that vein at all, not that I know of. Mind you, I doubt if they would reveal that side of things to me. A couple needs to have some privacy, don't they?"

"Quite right. But you think both their businesses were doing well?" Sam pressed.

"Yes, I'd say so, otherwise they wouldn't have been able to afford the new house. It was specifically designed for them, that must have cost a fortune," Cynthia said.

"And don't forget the cost of materials have escalated since the damn pandemic hit us," Mick added. "John told me he was gutted the house had ended up costing him nearly a third more than they had anticipated. But then, what a home they had. We would have easily swapped ours for it, wouldn't we, love?"

Cynthia shook her head. "Nope, not when you consider all the cleaning involved, I'd be at it all day." She pointed at her husband and whispered to Sam, "He's not the tidiest of men to live with."

Sam smiled. "Perhaps you can tell us if there's been any tension in the home lately?"

"Not that I can recall. John was the caring sort, he tried to alleviate as much pressure on Fiona as he could, to help with her recovery."

"Have they had any visitors to the house recently?"

"If they have then they haven't told me, and I haven't seen anyone new visiting them. They only tended to have John's parents around now and again, the rest of the time it was just the four of them. They devoted all their time to their kids, that's the way it should be as well, otherwise, why have kids in the first place?"

Sam kept her opinion to herself on that one, not having any motherly instincts of her own. "What about people hanging around outside the house, have you seen anyone while you were working?"

"I suppose there are still a few builders hanging around the site, they're completing the final house on the estate now."

"We'll go back and check once we're done here. Is there anything else you'd like to add before we leave?" Sam picked up her mug and finished her coffee while the couple contemplated their answer.

It was Cynthia who spoke first. "No, I don't think so. Hopefully, John will be able to help you out, if and when, he wakes up, although saying that, the injury to his head…" She swallowed, and fresh tears trickled onto her cheek. "I don't know enough about how the brain works, but it didn't look good to me. I dread to think what kind of life he's going to have, if he survives. Who the hell is going to care for him with his family all gone? Of course, Mick and I will do what we can, but by the looks of it, I think he's going to need special care that we just won't be able to offer."

"It's best not to think about that side of things. What we need to do is think positively and hope that he makes it," Sam said.

"Oh, I will, we will, but I'm fearful that his body won't be able to handle the trauma that it has been subjected to."

"It might be better if he doesn't pull through," Mick added quietly.

"Mick, how can you sit there and say that? Shame on you!" Cynthia reprimanded.

"Easily, with the injuries he's sustained, and what happens when he wakes up and finds out Fiona, Chrissie and Adam are all dead? How the dickens do you think he's going to feel about that? I'm putting myself in his position for a reason, love. I would rather be dead than have to contend with all of that, wouldn't you?"

Cynthia fell silent and sucked in a few deep breaths before she finally agreed with him. "I suppose you're right. What a mess. That poor family shred to pieces, and for what? Do you know what the person was after?"

Sam shook her head. "We don't. We've yet to determine if anything was missing from the house or what the killer's motive was. We will find out, though, you have my word."

"How?" Mick asked. "Do you even know how to begin the investigation? Were there any clues found at the house?"

"We're going to need to allow SOCO a few days to examine the premises before we can give a definitive answer, Mr Finch." She rose from her seat.

Bob slapped his notebook shut and followed her to the door.

"We can see ourselves out," Sam said. "Thank you for taking the time to speak with us. Again, we're sorry for your loss."

"Oh, wait, you need John's parents' address. I'll get that for you." Cynthia shot off the sofa and went to the back of the room, to a cabinet in the corner. She opened a drawer and riffled through a small notebook. Stopping at a page near the back, she tapped her finger. "Here it is. Thirty-two Needle Road, High Harrington. Do you know it?"

Sam nodded. "I know of it. We'll nip out there and see them. Thanks again for all the information you've given us today. Take care of each other."

"We will. Do your best for John, won't you?"

"Of course." Sam smiled and left the room.

Back in the car, Bob blew out a large breath. "That was tough. Nice couple. What do you think we're up against here?"

"I wish I knew. It's far too early to tell. Lots for us to do this morning, partner, none of it will be easy."

"Like breaking the news to his parents and then visiting him in hospital, if they'll allow us to see him."

"Exactly. I think the latter will need to be put on the back burner for now. While we're here, I think we should nip back to the scene, knock on a few doors, see what the neighbours can tell us."

He wagged a finger. "In other words, you need to build up the courage before heading over to see the parents."

Sam chewed on her lip. "Am I that easy to read?"

"Sometimes, yes. On this occasion I don't blame you, not one little bit. It's going to be tough breaking the news to the parents, especially given the father's heart condition."

"Yeah, that's why I need to weigh up what needs to be said before we head over there. So, we'll go back to the site and have a quick nosey around before we deploy uniform to complete the job for us."

"Makes sense to me."

Sam drove back to the crime scene, a knot of apprehension sitting in the pit of her stomach.

. . .

SHE PULLED up outside the last house on the estate. Several builders stood outside the property, looking over some plans.

"Are you going to have a word with them?" Bob asked, his hand hovering over the door handle.

"I think we should."

"And say what?"

She faced him and groaned. "Fucked if I know, but I can't *not* say anything either."

"Okay, I was only asking," Bob bit back.

"Well don't. You know the questions we ask, and who we interview, at the start of an investigation can be crucial in some cases."

"Yeah, it's the other few cases where it hasn't come to anything that's bugging me."

"Nonsense. Let's go. Want to split up?"

"Not particularly."

"Fine by me."

Bob grunted. "I'll take a step back and let you get on with it."

"Nothing different there then." Sam grinned and took pleasure in watching him squirm in his seat. She pushed open her door and got out of the vehicle.

The three men in high-vis jackets and hard hats glanced her way.

Sam produced her ID and said, "DI Sam Cobbs, and this is my partner, DS Bob Jones. Can you tell me who is in charge around here?"

"That would be me. I'm Jason Leigh, site manager."

"Pleased to meet you. Would it be all right if we had a quiet word somewhere?"

He pointed at a Portakabin within spitting distance of where they were standing. "My office is right here. What's this about? As if I couldn't guess."

Sam smiled. "We'll fill you in once we're inside."

"I'll catch up with you guys later, I shouldn't be too long."

The other two men went inside the house, and Jason led the way across the road and up the steps to his office.

"Come in, take a seat, if you can find one." He sat behind his desk, leaned back and placed his hands on top of his head.

Sam and Bob both chose to stand.

"Right, what can I do for you? The rumour mill has been in full swing since early this morning, but I'd rather get the facts from the horse's mouth, so to speak."

"I'm the same, don't care much for gossip, not in our line of work. You've probably heard that an incident occurred at the Wades' house over the weekend."

"Yeah, I did. We were shocked to see all the activity when we showed up for work today. Someone said lives were lost but couldn't tell me what had happened. Care to fill me in?"

"That's true. Three lives, and the husband is in hospital in a very serious condition."

"Jesus, how can I help?"

"I need to know if you have any cameras left on site?"

"We're in the process of dismantling everything at the moment. The cameras were taken out last Friday. We're due to complete the final house in the next few days. Head office told us to be prepared to leave. They want us off site by Wednesday at the latest."

"Why the rush?"

"Rush? No rush, time is money, as you can imagine. We've been on this site for over two years all told. The bosses are eager for us to move on to pastures new and start on the next project."

"Which is where?"

"About thirty miles north of here, up near Carlisle. Can't say I'm looking forward to it, travelling further from home every day."

"You live around here?"

"Not too far. It takes me approximately ten minutes to get to work. The new site is going to take me around forty minutes to get to, depending on the traffic, of course."

"What about the other staff you employ on site, are they all local, too?"

"Mostly. Those who come from further afield have been staying with some of the others, just because we're on a strict deadline."

"I see. Have you employed anyone new lately? In the past month or so?"

"Nope. I tend to stick with workmen I know and who I can rely on to get the job accomplished within the timescale."

"So the men on site have been here from day one. No strangers been seen around lately?"

"Not on my watch, lady."

"It's inspector, but I'll let you off this time."

"Sorry, that was rude of me, I apologise."

"Accepted. What we're trying to ascertain is whether someone new visited the site."

"Nope, I can categorically tell you there hasn't been anyone hanging around who isn't connected to the site. Even the delivery drivers have been the same ones we've used from when construction began."

"Then we'll be off. That's all we need to know. Thanks for speaking with us. Good luck with your next venture."

"Thanks. Can I ask who died?"

Sam shrugged. "It'll be on the news soon enough. The wife and two children. The husband received life-threatening injuries. We're not sure if he'll pull through or not."

He sat upright and placed his hands on the desk. "Shit. That's the worst news I'll hear all month. They were a nice family, really cool to work with. Didn't give my team much hassle during the construction phase or in the latter stages of the build. And you've got no idea who carried out the deed?

Obviously, otherwise you wouldn't be around here asking questions, would you?"

"Great observation on your part," Sam replied. "Thanks for your help. If any of your guys hear or see anything, will you give me a call?" She slid a card across the desk towards him.

"I will. Good luck, I mean it. They were a really nice family. I'm gutted to learn what has happened to them. They were so excited about living here. From a selfish point of view, I'm relieved about the timing."

Sam raised an eyebrow. "Meaning that had this crime been committed at the start of the build you would have had trouble selling the other properties on site?"

He tapped the side of his nose. "Correct. I can see nothing gets past you, Inspector."

"You're right, it doesn't. Wishing you a good day, Mr Leigh." She turned and walked out of the door.

Bob trotted to catch up with her. "Hey, where's the fire? He pissed you off, didn't he?"

"You could say that. Onwards and upwards."

They jumped back in the car and pulled up outside the crime scene once more.

Bob frowned and turned in his seat to face her. "I thought we were going to the parents' to break the news."

"Nope, you missed out the part where we knock on the immediate neighbours' doors and see what they have to say first."

He slapped his thigh. "Silly me."

"You take next door, and I'll see what the owners of the house opposite have to say. I've spotted a woman at the downstairs window, craning her neck to see what's going on."

"I noticed her, too. Okay, just the one neighbour?" He peered over his shoulder.

TO HOLD RESPONSIBLE

Sam did the same. The houses were angled in different directions, and Sam worked out that the house on the right had all its windows facing the wrong way for the owners to have seen anything. "Yeah, just the one. We'll revisit the estate if we have to. I'm going to ring the station, get them to flood the area ASAP, so for my peace of mind, we'll check the two main properties and then shoot over to the parents'. I can't put it off any longer, it wouldn't be right. I've already clocked the media circling. The last thing we need is for the parents to see the house on TV and get a shock that way."

"Yep, I hear you. See you in a tick."

They both left the car and went their separate ways.

The woman at the window left her viewing point and appeared at the front door to greet her. "You're the police, aren't you?"

Sam smiled and flashed her ID. "I am. And you are?"

"Lyn Thomas. I'm sorry, I would have come over when you arrived but... I'm not a well person and I don't get out much."

Sam inclined her head and stepped into the house as Lyn moved back into the hallway. "Are you telling me you suffer from agoraphobia?"

"Come in, can I get you a drink? Yes, that's right. I had an accident on a train a few years ago, and the result is this... that I'm now confined to the house, through no fault of my own. I sit there, every day at the lounge window, watching the world go by."

Excitement poked at Sam's gut. "What are you saying? That you see everything that goes on out there, day and night?"

The woman's blue eyes sparkled under the hallway lights. "Come through to the lounge, and I'll show you what I mean."

Sam removed her shoes rather than dirty the woman's

obviously new carpet with possible mud from the messy location she'd come from at the rear. She followed Lyn into the lounge.

The room was larger than Sam anticipated. She was glad to see the woman had decorated her home properly, unlike the Wades who had left theirs stark white.

Sam sat on the cream sofa. "You have a beautiful home."

"Thank you. Do you like the colour? I'm not sure the coffee is right for in here." The woman's hands shook, and she clasped them together in her lap. "Would you believe this is the fourth colour I've chosen for this room since I moved in a year ago?"

"Oh my. I would struggle changing the décor that much, it's my least favourite DIY job."

"Mine, too, but sitting here all day, often staring at these four walls, can drive me nuts, so out comes the paintbrush, and this is the result."

"It's lovely. Warm and welcoming."

"I thought so when I first did it, but now, I'm fed up with it."

"How long has it been like this?"

"Six days and counting," Lyn said and pulled a face. "Still, you haven't come here to discuss my bad taste in the colour chart. How can I help?"

Sam's gaze drifted towards the window. "I take it you're aware of what has happened across the road."

Lyn gestured at the dining chair sitting in the bay window. "I have the perfect view. I watched them take the bodies away. I'm presuming the wife and the kids lost their lives because I also saw the ambulance arrive to collect the husband. Am I correct?"

"One hundred percent. I have to ask if you saw anyone hanging around the house over the weekend."

"Not as such. On the Saturday night, the family ordered a

takeaway which was delivered by a man on a bike, or should I say a moped?" Her brow furrowed, and her gaze drifted to the window once more.

"Is there something else?"

"I'm wondering if the bike was the same one I saw parked up outside their property later on Saturday night."

Sam's interest piqued to another level. She withdrew her notebook and jotted down the information while still studying the pained expression distorting Lyn's features. "It would be helpful if you could be sure. I know it's not much, but clues are limited at the moment, and every snippet we can pick up now will help our investigation."

"I'm trying to think. Give me a second or two." Lyn closed her eyes and opened them wide a few moments later. "Yes, I can see it clearly now. It was larger than the delivery guy's, much larger."

"Can you describe it for me? What colour was it?"

"It was a dark blue and had a silver stripe on the paintwork. I'm sorry, I can't do better than that. I'm not certain what the part is called, I prefer four wheels to two."

"Don't worry, I know what you mean. I don't suppose you caught the numberplate, or part of it?"

"Hang on, let me think about that for a second." She closed her eyes again and nodded. "Yes, it consisted of the numbers one, two and three, in that order, but as far as the letters go, I'm sorry, I don't have a clue."

"It's okay. Let's move on, maybe something will come to you during our conversation."

"I hope so."

"What time was the bike at the house, can you remember?"

"I think around nine o'clock or thereabouts. I was considering going to bed because the TV was abysmal. I read quite a lot, you see, love my Kindle, either that or I buy paperbacks online if they're reduced, what with me not being able to get out."

"I have a Kindle, too. Best invention ever, isn't it? So around nine? Any idea how long it remained parked up?"

"I don't know for sure but I would hazard a guess around fifteen to twenty minutes. I thought they must have a visitor. Don't tell me that's the person who committed the crime?"

Sam shrugged. "It's the only lead we have to go on at the moment. Can you tell me anything about the driver? Did you see them?"

"I nipped to put the kettle on to make a cocoa to take to bed, and when I returned, I saw the person mount the bike and roar away on it. Noisy bloody things, they are. Can't you lot do something about the peace those contraptions disturb?"

Sam smiled. "I wish. They get to me as well. Most of them have been adapted in some way so they're far noisier than when they left the factory. The driver?"

"Ah, yes. Their build was that of a slim man. I think I would be right in saying that it wasn't a woman. Men are built differently, aren't they? He was very slender with skinny legs. He wore a helmet, so I can't tell you his hair colour or if he had any facial hair, like a beard, sorry."

"Don't be. This is excellent, you're doing well. Anything else?"

Lyn closed her eyes again as she thought. "His leathers were black, I don't know if that's relevant or not. Aren't all leathers black?"

"I'm not sure. I'll note it down just in case. And the helmet, what colour was that?"

"Either black or perhaps a navy blue. It was a darker one, not light at all, if that helps?"

"It does. You're doing great. Anything else? Did the

leathers have any markings on them? Any stickers on the bike, that sort of thing?"

She opened her eyes and shook her head. "No, I don't think so, not that I can recall."

Sam stood and glanced out of the window. "You can see the main road from here. Did you happen to notice which direction the bike took?"

"Yes, to the right, I'm sure of it."

"Great. Have you ever seen the bike around here before?"

Lyn's mouth twisted as she contemplated the question. She clicked her finger and thumb together. "Why yes, maybe it was last week or possibly the week before, there was another noisy motorbike on the estate. I thought it was someone to do with the house they're getting ready at the back of the estate, but maybe not. Do you think it could be the same person? Possibly seeing how the land lies, you know, staking the estate out, isn't that what the cops call it?"

Sam smiled. "Maybe in America. Watch a lot of TV from there, do you?"

"Oh my, guilty as charged."

Sam scanned the notes she'd made and then looked Lyn in the eye and asked, "And you've only seen this bike twice in the past what, couple of weeks?"

"Yes, I don't think it was any more than that. Did the family suffer before they died?"

"I can't tell you that, I'm afraid. It's not that I don't want to, it's simply because I don't know. I would hope not, considering gas had been used."

"Gas? Someone left the gas on, is that it? Why didn't the house explode?"

"No, the killer used a crude gas canister, the type used by the army."

"How strange. Seems a little extreme, doesn't it?"

"I agree. It takes all sorts to make up this despicable world of ours."

"It's getting worse, isn't it? A horrible world we live in when a family is torn apart like that. They were such a nice family, too. The mother and father, not sure of their names, they always waved to me when they saw me. I bet they thought I was a right nosey bugger, sitting here all day, watching everything that goes on in the estate."

Sam smiled at the woman who she presumed was in her mid- to late thirties. "Are you getting any help?"

"Yes, I have a therapist who comes to visit me once a month, not sure the treatment is helping much at all."

"Private or NHS?"

"NHS."

"I might know someone who would be willing to see you privately. He's wonderful to work with, I can thoroughly recommend him."

"Connected to the police, is he?"

Sam nodded. "In a way. I'll give you one of his cards. Tell him I sent you."

Lyn read out the name on the card. "Rhys Wilkins. I've not heard of him."

"He's relatively new to the area and a good man, from what I've heard."

"I'll give him a ring. Some of these people don't make home visits, though, or if they do, they charge the earth for them."

"Mention my name, it'll work wonders, guaranteed."

"I will, and thank you."

"My pleasure. Was there anything else you wanted to share with me before I leave?"

"No, except to pass on my condolences to the family. I've seen an older couple visit there now and again. The man always seems a little fragile in my opinion."

"That's probably John's mother and father. The lady who cleans for them told us earlier that the father is in poor health. That's our next stop, to break the news to them."

"Oh no, how awful. What a thing to be told. I wouldn't want your job for all the tea in China."

"It has its moments. Right, thank you so much for taking the time to speak with me. I'm sure the information you have given me will come in useful during the investigation."

They walked back to the front door, and Sam slipped on her shoes.

"And give Rhys a call. He's a genuinely nice guy."

"I'm sensing there is more between you than just a professional relationship, am I right?"

Sam grinned. "I couldn't possibly comment. Mention my name, though, he might even offer you a discount."

"Sounds good to me. Thank you again. I hope the information I've given you does help."

"I hope so, too. Take care of yourself, Lyn."

Lyn closed the door behind Sam. She walked back to the car. Bob was still questioning the neighbour next door. He gave a cursory glance her way.

Sam slid into the driver's seat and rang the station. "Hi, Claire, it's me. I've got a brief update for you. We've interviewed the Wades' cleaner. She told us that John Wade ran an export business in the area. Can you do some research for me? I also spoke to the neighbour across the road who said she saw a motorbike sitting outside the Wades' home around nineish on Saturday evening. Can you see if we can find any ANPRs or CCTV footage for this area? It's a new estate, so I'm not holding out much hope."

"Leave it with me, I'll see what I can gather."

"Also, the crime scene is a little sketchy at the moment, but it would appear the three family members who died were all gassed. There was a gas canister found in the family cinema room. The pathologist is under the impression that it might have been tampered with to make it even more lethal, if that's possible. What I need to know is how readily available these canisters are. I'm going to forward a photo of it that I took at the scene."

"That would be helpful, thanks, boss. Again, I'll do some digging, or do you want me to pass that task on to one of the others to research for you?"

"Yes, good idea. You have enough to do as it is. See if Oliver will take the task on. No, wait, let Alex do it, he's ex-military. He might have some contacts he can call on."

"Sounds like a plan. Will do. Anything else you need, boss?"

"No, the priority is to find out what we can about the business, Claire, and the motorbike element as well. We're on our way to visit the husband's mother and father now, I'm dreading it. After that, we'll return to base."

"Good luck, you have a tough job ahead of you."

"Thanks, don't I know it?" Sam ended the call.

At the same time Bob jumped into the passenger seat beside her. "Bloody hell, I didn't think I was ever going to get away from that bloke."

"Why?"

"I reckon he brought up every subject under the sun. He'd win a contest for incessant talker, hands down, if they ever held one."

"Ah, but did he give you any decent information? Anything we can work with?"

"Nope, absolutely zilch. He got enough out of me, though. Wanted to know the ins and outs of a duck's arse."

Sam laughed. "And you told him in the hope that he would be able to give you something useful in return."

"Yeah, go on, take the mickey out of me."

Sam slapped a hand over her chest. "Would I?"

"Yeah, you would. Anyway, how did you get on? I see you got invited in, whereas I had to conduct my interview on the doorstep."

"I have a way with people, you don't. I'll fill you in en route. Can you punch the information into the satnav for me?"

"I'll ignore that dig. I do my best. If it's not good enough…"

"Stop wallowing in self-pity and get on with the task in hand."

CHAPTER 2

The house was a small semi on the edge of High Harrington, close to the school.

"I bet this is noisy during the day," Sam said.

"You're not kidding. I've been around here when the school kicks out, and it's bedlam, pure and simple," Bob agreed.

"Poor people. I bet they were envious of where their son lived."

They got out of the car and entered the front garden of the house.

Bob pointed out a *For Sale* sign that had possibly fallen over in the high winds they'd suffered lately. "Probably. Maybe there were plans for them moving out to be closer to the son."

"Ouch, yes, maybe you're right. Okay, brace yourself."

"I'm fully braced and glad to be leaving all the talking to you."

"Nothing new there." Sam rang the bell.

The door was answered a few seconds later by a man in his seventies. Sam noted his breathing wasn't the best.

"Hello, sir. I'm DI Sam Cobbs, and this is my partner, DS Bob Jones. Would it be okay if we come in for a chat with you and your wife? Is she in?"

"The police? What's this about?"

"It would be better if we spoke to you both at the same time, sir."

"You'd better come in then. Iris, the police are here to see us," he called over his shoulder and dipped back behind the inner door.

A woman of a similar age appeared in a doorway off to the left. "The police? Has something happened? It's bad, isn't it? I just know it is."

Sam nodded. "Can we come in?"

"Yes, of course. Bert, you need to get your medication, just in case."

"What? Are you serious?" he asked, perplexed.

"Maybe it would be for the best, Mr Wade," Sam confirmed.

He ascended the stairs behind him while Mrs Wade showed them through to the lounge.

"I'm having a sort-out. Our paperwork is in a mess, thought I'd spend ten minutes going through it. That was a couple of hours ago. Can I get you both a drink?"

Sam smiled. "We're fine. I tend to shove all my paperwork in a drawer at home until I get the chance to file it properly. I think mine is long overdue."

Mr Wade entered the room. They all took a seat; the couple sat on the sofa, and Sam and Bob on the two armchairs opposite them.

"Come on, out with it," Mr Wade demanded, not allowing Sam to take a breath to prepare herself.

"I'm sorry, the news isn't good. This morning we were called to your son's house over in Stainburn…"

She paused to search for the appropriate words to finish her sentence, but Mr Wade jumped in impatiently.

"And? What are you here to tell us?"

Sam exhaled. "Unfortunately, well, there's no easy way to say this, but…"

"Spit it out," Mr Wade insisted.

"Now, Bert, keep that temper of yours under control, you know what the doctor told you about getting uptight."

"It's not me you should be having a pop at, it's her. Tell her to get on with it."

Sam took the hint and persevered. "It's with great sadness that I have to tell you your son and his family were subjected to an attack over the weekend."

"What? No, this can't be happening," Mrs Wade slapped a hand over her mouth and shook her head.

"What are you telling us?" Mr Wade's eyes narrowed. "Attack, what sort of attack? Was their house broken into?"

"We believe that to be the case, yes. Your son was found in the kitchen with life-threatening injuries."

"He what? This can't be right. I knew they shouldn't have had that house built, flaunting their wealth in that manner, it's not the done thing. Didn't I tell him?" Mr Wade asked his wife.

"I'm not going to answer that, Bert, you and I both know what has been said regarding the subject, now is not the time for recriminations. I need to know what my son and his family have been subjected to. I tried to ring them over the weekend. I got no response so presumed they'd gone away somewhere. Sometimes they take off, leave their phones on silent and enjoy the time together. Please, tell me what's happened to them. I need to know."

"Your son is in hospital, he's unconscious. Sadly, his wife and your two grandchildren didn't survive."

Iris reached for her husband's hand, clearly stunned by the news.

It was up to Mr Wade to ask more questions, "What? They're dead? How? Do you know who did this? Have you caught them yet?"

"Sorry, one question at a time. Your son was found in a different area of the house. Your daughter-in-law and grandchildren were in the home cinema, we presume watching a film."

"Yes, yes, they mentioned they were going to see *Maverick* over the weekend, I've just remembered!" Mrs Wade said. "Why didn't I think about that when I couldn't get hold of them? This is too shocking for words. Dead... how can they be dead? At their age. This is..."

"All right, love. No matter what spin you put on it, it amounts to the same thing... they're gone."

Those words jolted both of them. Mr Wade flung an arm around his wife's shoulders, and they openly sobbed together. Sam and Bob remained quiet in the awkward situation which lasted a good ten minutes. Eventually, Mr Wade gently pushed his wife away from him and kissed her on the nose.

"We need to be strong, for John's sake. He'll be relying on us to get him through this. We won't be able to do that if we crumble at the first hurdle, love, will we?"

"I know, but the thought of never laying eyes on the three of them again, hugging them, sharing laughter-filled moments with Chrissie and Adam... oh my, I can't bring myself to think about it. Why them? Why two innocent teenagers? How is that right?" Iris said on another sob.

"What leads do you have?" Mr Wade asked.

"After speaking with one of your son's neighbours, she has given us a huge lead to chase up," Sam said.

"Which is?" Mr Wade asked, his tone getting more impatient with every question.

"She saw a motorbike parked outside your son's house at around nine o'clock on Saturday night. Do you know who it might belong to?"

"Should I, we? Of course we don't. Our son leads his own life, he doesn't need to report to us every time someone drops by the house for a visit."

"I understand that. It was a hopeful request more than anything. I am going to need to ask you some very personal questions about the family, in the hope that will open some new avenues for us to investigate, will that be okay with you?"

Iris reached for her husband's hand again. She looked lost and vulnerable to Sam, and her heart went out to the woman.

"I think so. We'll do our best to answer as accurately as possible, not that we know everything about our son's life," Iris said. "He left home over twenty years ago. When children do that, they tend to only tell their parents what they want to hear, in case you're unaware. We're not nosey people as a rule. John knows he can turn to us if he's ever in trouble, but as far as anything else is concerned, he got on with taking care of his family, with Fiona's help, of course."

"I totally get that. Perhaps you can tell me what sort of export business your son ran?"

"Exporting goods abroad, that's usually what's involved, isn't it?" Mr Wade chipped in.

"Any idea what type of goods and where they're exported to?"

Mr Wade shrugged. "Not a bloody clue. Is that why you think they were killed?"

Sam shook her head. "It's hard to tell at this stage, but it seems an obvious place to start our investigation."

"I think you're right," Iris said. "However, we know very little about his business, he didn't confide in us that much."

"Okay. Do you know if John has made any enemies over the years?"

"Probably, we all do, don't we?" Mr Wade replied, his tone off-hand.

"I can't say I have, not really," Sam responded. *Except for Chris, and do ex-husbands count? Not that he was an ex-husband when he died.*

"Aren't you lucky? I would have thought coppers would make dozens of enemies during their time in the Force."

"Depends if they carry out their roles properly or not, I suppose. Can you tell me if Fiona and John had a happy marriage? To your knowledge, did either of them have an affair?"

Iris tutted. "Not a chance. They were devoted to each other. They loved one another even more once the children were born, it never dwindled like for some couples. My friend's daughter was divorced within six months of having her child. The husband couldn't stand the responsibility of being a father and cheated on her. She caught him at it in the car with his secretary when she surprised him one day while he was at work."

"Ouch, that must have hurt."

"It did. John adored his kids, made sure he spent most of his spare time with them, unlike some fathers I know who are self-employed."

"Am I right in thinking that Fiona ran a boutique in Workington?"

"That's right, with one of her best friends. They started it up about ten years ago, I believe. She got bored of being at home every day once Adam started playschool, and John put his hand in his pocket and lent her the money to kit out the shop. See, our son is a good man, which begs the question, why someone would deliberately go out of their way to punish John and his family like this. None of it is making any sense to me."

Iris buried her head in her hands, and Mr Wade pulled her close and held her head against his chest.

"There, there, love. We'll get through this, we always do."

"Always do? Has something of this magnitude happened within your family before, Mr Wade?" Sam asked, determined not to let his comment pass by unnoticed.

"No, definitely not. I meant we've had life-changing news to deal with before and have coped."

"Such as?"

"Both our parents were killed in a plane crash back in the nineties. They often travelled abroad on holiday together, they became great friends after we got married, so much so that they died together."

"I'm sorry to hear that. Where were they travelling to?"

Mr Wade shook his head, and tears welled up. "It's that long ago I can't bloody remember, can you, love?"

"It was somewhere in Africa. There was a great deal of terrorist activity in the area. The plane was shot down when it passed over a certain area, wiping out all the passengers and crew. They didn't stand a chance. We're grateful they went quickly and didn't have to suffer the trauma of dealing with lost limbs et cetera, as happens in a lot of cases of this nature. Our hearts broke that day. We believe that event was the reason Bert now has heart problems."

"I'm sorry to hear that, Mr Wade," Sam said genuinely. "It must have been a nightmare situation to deal with."

"It was, an international cock-up of massive proportions. The UK were hopeless, didn't have a bloody clue. I have very little faith in anything connected to the British Government when I hear they're involved in releasing hostages in another country. They're worse than useless, rarely get the job done without recriminations. As for the police…"

"Now, Bert, stop it. We need to have faith in the inspector and her team. I'm sure she won't let us down, not intentionally. Will you, dear?" Iris asked.

"I'm not in the habit of letting families down, neither is my team. However, for us to get started on the investigation we're going to need some insight into the family's characters and the lives they led."

"As for characters, you couldn't wish for a better son, daughter-in-law and grandchildren," Iris insisted. "They never forgot either of our birthdays and always made a genuine effort to either spend Christmas with us or involve us in their plans. Who could ask for more than that?"

"What about Fiona's family?"

"Her father walked out on her when she was three, and her mother died when she was seven, so her aunt brought her up as her own."

"Does she live in the area?"

Iris swallowed and shook her head. "No, she died a few years ago from breast cancer. She was Fiona's only living relative. That's why she went above and beyond for her own family. I got the sense that she felt she missed out as a child and was desperate to ensure the same thing didn't happen to her own children. She was a wonderful mother. Yes, she ran her own business, but she did everything she could not to let work get in the way of her family life. She bent over backwards for the children. They weren't spoilt as such but they did have everything they needed. The after-school clubs they attended were intended to mould their futures. Chrissie was serious about being a pianist, she even has a signed picture of Elton John on her bedroom wall. He cared enough about her to reply to a message she sent him, telling him how much she enjoyed his work. As we've already said, the kids were a different class to normal kids."

"Yes, Cynthia said exactly the same. She couldn't praise them highly enough."

Iris frowned. "Who is Cynthia?"

"The cleaner. She was the lady who found the family and placed the nine-nine-nine call."

"Ah, yes, of course. I should have remembered. The memory plays tricks on me now and again, so you'll have to forgive me. Have you seen our son?"

"Not yet. I didn't think there was any point in going to the hospital, we were told he was in a bad way and unconscious. Therefore, I thought it would be better to get the ball rolling on the investigation. Interview as many people as we can today, and then I'll visit your son tomorrow."

"I see. Who have you spoken to so far?" Iris asked.

"The neighbours, the site manager on the estate, Cynthia and yourselves."

"And have you learnt anything of value?" Mr Wade asked.

"I think so. We know there was the motorbike at the property. All we need to do now is find the owner and interview them in order to ascertain why they were at the property."

"What about cameras in the area?" Mr Wade asked.

"I've got my team going through all the relevant footage to see what shows up. Unfortunately, your son didn't have any security cameras fitted at the house, do you know why?"

"Simple, he didn't believe in them, not at home. At work it was a different matter entirely."

"Talking of which, can you tell us the name of his business or the address of where we can find the office?"

"Yes, it's called… damn, I've forgotten, it's on the tip of my tongue. Hang on, I should have a card somewhere." Mr Wade left his seat and returned with a business card that he handed to Bob.

"Worldwide Exports," Bob read out.

"I suppose that answers my question about which country he exports to," Sam said. "Is there an address on there, Bob?"

"Term Bank Industrial Estate, Workington. I think I know where it is. I'll check on Google Maps."

Sam left him to it. "Does your son run the business alone?"

"Yes, that's right," Mr Wade replied after taking his seat again. "There was talk of him searching for someone to go in with him as the business was expanding rapidly. Not sure if that came to fruition or not, you'll have to check."

"Thanks, we'll look into it. Is there anything else you'd like to share with us before we go?"

The Wades shook their heads in unison.

"Will we be able to see our son? Do we just show up at the hospital?" Iris asked, fear settling in her eyes for the first time during the interview as the realisation set in.

"Of course you will. I can ring the hospital, see what ward he's on for you, if you like. Although, I think he's most likely to be in Intensive Care, given his injuries."

"Oh my, yes, if you wouldn't mind. We'll try and get our heads around it after you leave and get over there when we can."

"I'll do it in the hallway." Sam rose from her seat and left the room. She rang the hospital at Whitehaven, only to be told that someone with John's serious injuries would be transferred to Carlisle Hospital right away. Sam groaned inside. That would make her job a whole lot harder from the outset. She wouldn't be able to visit him, there would be no point, not until he regained consciousness. Carlisle was at least an hour's journey away, two if you counted the return journey. That was a considerable amount of time to be away from the investigation. She rang the ICU at Carlisle and was told that John had arrived, he was being monitored closely, and that the doctor was hesitant about giving a prognosis as to whether he was going to make it or not.

Damn, how the hell do I tell the parents that?

Sucking in a steadying breath, Sam returned to the lounge to reveal a brief summary of the news she'd been given.

"Unfortunately, your son has been transferred to Carlisle Hospital because Whitehaven isn't equipped to deal with such traumas."

"Heck, how the hell are we supposed to get up there, to be with him until he wakes up?" Mr Wade said.

"We'll have to pack a bag. I can drive there, it's not a problem, Bert. Don't put obstacles in our way, not when our son's life hangs in the balance."

"I didn't mean to. It's the inconvenience of it all. This area sucks for emergency cover. Not everyone can lay their hands on transport these days, and you can't rely on the rail service, not with all these strikes taking place. It's such a bloody mess." His hands slapped either side of his face. "What a mess," he repeated. "Our son's life is teetering on the edge, and we're forty-odd miles away from him. He needs us to be with him, day in day out, until he recovers, and they do this to us."

Iris sought out his hand and gathered it in her own. "It is what it is, there's no point in us complaining about it. We've just got to do our best for him. Now stop thinking negatively all the time. It's imperative we remain upbeat and positive."

"I was just stating the facts as I see them, love. I would never dream of being negative in front of him. The poor lad is going to need our strength to pull him through this."

"I know. He's going to need our support more than ever. Oh God, I forgot about Jessica."

Sam tilted her head. "Who's that?"

"His sister, our daughter. I should ring her, let her know what's happened. Can I do that now?"

"Fine by me," Sam confirmed.

Iris picked up the mobile sitting on the side table and punched in a number. "Hello, love. I have some bad news for you. Are you sitting down…? I'm not being over dramatic, Jess. Give me a chance to tell you. Are you ready now? Okay, please don't argue with me, this is hard enough as it is… Be patient with me, I know you don't possess much patience at the best of times." Iris rolled her eyes at her husband.

He tried to wrench the phone out of her hand, but Iris turned her back on him.

"Listen to me, Jessica, no, I insist. I'm just going to come out and say it then. There have been three deaths in the family, have I got your attention now…? Thank you. Not everything is about you…! I'm sorry, no, I shouldn't have said that, but you forced my hand. There's more… Your brother is in hospital, fighting for his life… That's what I said… you need to know all the facts. Are you prepared to listen to me now? I'll tell you the full story, but you're going to have to stop interrupting me." Iris leaned against her husband for support as if drawing on his strength.

"This is what happened."

Sam watched Iris regain her composure and tell her daughter the facts as she knew them. Sam couldn't help but feel sorry for the trauma Iris had decided to put herself through, making the call. She smiled every time the woman glanced up at her, Iris's frustration all too clear in her attempt to inform her daughter.

"Thank you for allowing me to speak. Are you all right? Yes, your father and I are coping… just. Don't give me that… of course we're bloody upset, our whole family, or most of them, have been slaughtered. It'll probably hit us harder when we show up at the hospital and see what condition John is in... Yes, the inspector in charge of the investigation and her partner are with us now. So far they've been excellent. No, I'm not going to pass the phone over so you can speak to her. We're dealing with the situation, there's no need for you to stick your oar in." Iris held the phone away from her ear. The room filled with her daughter's voice shouting down the line. Iris pressed the End Call button and switched her phone off at the side. "I've had it with her selfish behaviour. You can deal with her if she calls back, Bert."

He tutted. "The trouble is, you two get off on winding each other up. She's bound to be upset by the news, she and John are very close."

"Stop treating me like an outsider, I'm aware of the dynamics of this family. I also know that you refuse to have a single word said against her."

Mr Wade jumped to his feet and marched out of the room.

Iris withdrew a tissue from the box close by and sobbed. "Damn them both. They're like two peas in a pod. Father and daughter relationships suck sometimes, especially when they erect barriers that others find impossible to break down. I've had more problems with Jessica over the years than I care to remember. She's the type who always needs to be the centre of attention. Well, I can tell you, that no longer washes with me, not with what's at stake right now."

"I'm sorry she reacted that way to the news. Maybe it was the grief talking."

Iris raised an eyebrow and snorted. "It wasn't, the damn woman has always been the same, selfish and just... just... plain ignorant most of the time. Strike up a conversation with her, and worse has happened to her only the week before or she's done much better than you at something. She never lets up, it drives me potty. Like I said, I'll let Bert deal with her because I'm incapable of doing it, that much is obvious."

"Maybe she'll come round to your way of thinking once the news has sunk in."

"She won't. She's forty-five and she won't be changing anytime soon, I can guarantee it."

"Is she married?" Sam asked.

"Yes, to a lovely man, Patrick. Irish, he is, a great sense of humour. Not sure what he's doing with Jessica. Ouch, that was a bit harsh. Forgive me, I'm very upset, and sometimes her moods and attitude can bring out the worst in me."

"There's no need for you to apologise. Does Jessica live locally?"

"Yes, a few miles down the road. We see more of her and her family than we do of John, since they made the move out to Stainburn. I know I shouldn't say this, but I wish it was the other way around. That's why we're in the process of selling up, so that we can move closer to John and further away from Jessica. That's causing friction between us. She's always accusing me of putting John first. I suppose I have over the years, only because of Jessica's attitude towards me."

"A catch-twenty-two situation, I should imagine."

"You're not wrong there. I wish I had my time over, made more effort with her when she was in her teens, but she was utterly terrible to deal with. No compassion for anyone else, very self-centred. Bert made things ten times worse by giving in to her most of the time."

"Like you say, father and daughter relationships can be detrimental to the family unit more often than not."

"Yes, I agree, they force them apart. If I could live my life again, I wouldn't have allowed her to be so dominant in her teens. She used to seek out trouble, I'm sure of it, if only to wind me up. We spent a lot of time at the police station, collecting her. All minor incidences, of course, shoplifting, drinking on street corners with the gang she used to hang out with. Whereas John, he never did anything wrong. He brought his children up the right way as well."

"Does Jessica have any children of her own?"

"Yes, Marnie. I'm afraid she has her moments, too, just like her mother. How Patrick puts up with their shenanigans I will never know, he's such a placid, likeable man. I think that's where the problem lies. He lets them get away with it, so he has a peaceful life."

"She might call back and speak to your husband. Maybe as things stand, it's time to put all the past behind you and move on. You're going to be relying on your daughter and your husband to get you through this. John is going to need all his relatives around him, once he regains consciousness."

Iris fell quiet. By her expression, Sam wondered if the woman whose heart was breaking was having second thoughts about her daughter.

They sat there for a couple of minutes until the sitting room door burst open and a woman in her forties, with dyed red hair, marched towards Iris who appeared stunned to see her. Sam felt the need to intervene and prevented the new arrival getting too close to Iris.

"Stop right there."

"And who the fuck are you to tell me to keep away from my own mother?"

"I take it you're Jessica."

"That's right. You have me at a disadvantage. You are?"

Sam produced her warrant card. "DI Sam Cobbs. Why don't we all take a seat and discuss what's going on without raising our voices at each other?"

"And why don't you mind your own damn business?" Jessica sneered, her head jutting forward into Sam's personal space. "I have a score to settle with my mother and I'd prefer it if you left the room."

Sam stood her ground. "It's not going to happen. We were in the same room when your mother spoke to you. I've been half expecting you to show up. To kick off by what your mother has told me about your relationship with each other. I'm sorry, but I'm not going to sit back and allow you to get heavy handed with her."

Jessica crossed her arms and tapped her foot. "Is that so? And what exactly do you propose doing about it?"

"What's necessary, *believe* me. Your mother deserves respect, especially today, when she's dealing with the aftermath of a horrendous crime that has robbed her of half her family."

"Respect? After the way she spoke to me earlier? Where's her respect for me? You don't know us, or the type of shit I've had to contend with over the years, dealing with my mother's hatred for me."

"What? How ridiculous of you to think that way," Iris shouted, horrified. "Nothing could be further from the truth. Go find your father. I want him to listen to the putrid tripe that is spilling out of your mouth."

As if on cue, Mr Wade entered the room and seemed shocked to see his daughter confronting his wife. "Jessica? What are you doing here? Oh no, don't tell me you've come to cause trouble for your mother? How dare you? Take two steps back. I can tell when you mean business, my girl. Don't think you can wrap me around your finger, *not* today. It's time you started listening to your mother and stop disrespecting her."

"But, Dad," Jessica whined. "You didn't hear the way she spoke to me on the phone earlier."

"I did because I was sitting right next to your mother. You

refused to allow her to speak, preferring to hear the sound of your own voice, as usual."

Jessica's mouth hung open. After a few seconds, she whispered, "Dad, how can you speak to me that way?"

"Easily. Perhaps I should have done it years ago. Your mother's right, how dare you come round here shouting the odds! It's impertinent and utterly inappropriate because of what's happened to John and his family."

Jessica's head sank low, and her shoulders dipped in defeat. Sam's guard dropped at the same time.

"Now sit down and listen to what your mother has to say, for once in your life," he added, his tone holding a warning if she refused.

Sam couldn't help but feel proud about the way he appeared to be finally sticking up for his wife, something he'd neglected to do in the past.

"I think we should all take a seat to continue this conversation," Sam agreed.

The challenging glare Jessica had used on Sam and her mother when she had entered the room had diminished and was now replaced by sheepish embarrassment. "I'm sorry," she eventually mumbled and sat on the sofa next to her mother. "You mentioned Fiona and the children all died, how? Did John do this to his family? Why is he in hospital?"

Sam jumped in before Jessica's parents had the chance to fly off the handle at the accusation. "No, John was found in a separate room to his family. Your brother is in a bad way, we're not sure yet if he's going to make it."

Jessica repeatedly shook her head. "This can't be right. How can something like this occur? In a separate room, you said, so they were at home? Did someone break in?"

"We believe so, yes. SOCO and the pathologist are examining the crime scene as we speak. Their extensive examination will last for a few days."

"I can't believe this. Mum, I'm so sorry for my childish behaviour. How can I ever make it up to you?"

"It doesn't matter. You're here now and you've apologised. Let's move on and forget about what's gone on in the past. We have much more important things to worry about in our immediate future. Your brother has been whisked off to Carlisle Hospital. We've only just found out, we were in the middle of sorting out how to get there, but first, I wanted to give you a call to make you aware of the situation," Iris told her daughter.

"And I acted like a two-year-old, spitting my dummy out, as usual. You didn't need that. I regret my actions; can you ever forgive me?"

"It's done. We won't mention it again. How are you fixed for travelling to Carlisle? I haven't driven in a while, and your father's ill health means they've suspended his licence for the next few months."

"Goodness, I'd forgotten about that. I can have a word with Patrick, I'm sure he won't mind me borrowing the family car to take you up there. He can catch the bus home, or walk, it's not that far. I'd better get in touch with him to break the news." She leapt to her feet and left the room.

Sam studied the husband and wife, the relief palpable.

"Thank you for standing your ground with her," Iris said. She touched her husband's face with her right hand.

"I would always stand by you in a troubled storm, my love. It's imperative we show a united front. Let's hope this is the start of new beginnings, for all of us. I know that seems a weird thing to say at a time like this, with our son's life in imminent danger."

Iris smiled. "I understand what you mean. I'm sorry you had to witness that, Inspector. It disrupted our conversation, Jessica bursting into the room like that. Where were we?"

"There's no need to apologise. I think we're almost done

here now. Your priority remains with your son. The sooner you can get to the hospital to see him the better. We don't want to hold you up any longer than we need to. We'll do the necessary digging about what we've learnt so far and go from there. Now, is there anything you need to ask me before we leave?"

"No, I don't think so. Except to ask if you will keep us informed, during the investigation," Iris said after a slight pause.

"That goes without saying. We're going to head off, if that's okay with you."

Sam and Bob rose to their feet once more and walked towards the door which opened before they got there.

Jessica stopped in front of them. "Patrick has given me the all-clear to pick the car up. A taxi will be here soon. I'll go and collect it then pop back here to collect you. Are you ready to go? Do you need to pack an emergency overnight bag just in case?"

"That's a good idea," Iris said. She stood and tottered a little unsteadily.

Mr Wade jumped up and grabbed his wife's elbow.

"Thank you, dear. Sod this getting old malarky."

Sam bid them farewell, and Bob followed her to the front door. Jessica accompanied them while her mother and father waved and ascended the stairs together.

"Do your best for my family, Inspector. I apologise if we got off on the wrong foot."

"Don't worry, we've come across far worse reactions from family members in similar circumstances. Just look after your mother and father. I get the sense that it hasn't really sunk in with them yet."

"Don't worry, I'll be with them every step of the way from now on."

A thud sounded overhead.

"Mum, Dad, is everything all right up there?" Jessica shouted, frantically.

"No, it's your father, call an ambulance," Iris bellowed, distraught. "I think he's had a heart attack."

"Shit. Where's my damn phone?" Jessica said in a flap.

"Go, see if you can help your mother. Bob, go with her. I'll make the call."

Bob bolted up the stairs, two at a time, ahead of Jessica. Sam paced the hallway and dialled nine-nine-nine. The operator answered immediately.

"Hi, I need an ambulance. I'm DI Sam Cobbs of the Cumbria Constabulary. I'm at the scene and I believe Mr Bert Wade, the homeowner, has suffered a heart attack."

"Okay, have you seen the patient yourself?"

"Not yet. I've just delivered some bad news to the family and I thought he was okay. They went upstairs to pack an overnight bag in preparation for a hospital visit, and he collapsed. He has a bad heart and has struggled in recent months. Please, can you send the ambulance right away?" She reeled off the address.

"It's been dispatched. If you can give me any further details, it would make life easier, and I can pass the information on to the crew."

"I believe I've told you everything. Wait, my partner is up there. Let me see what's happening. Bob, how is he?"

Bob came into view at the top of the stairs, shrugged and held his arms out to the side.

"Shit! I think it's too late. Please, hurry, they might be able to save him."

"Let me see how far away they are. Crap, it's going to be ten minutes, maybe fifteen before they get to you. Can you try and do CPR on the patient? I'll guide you through it."

"I'm not sure I'm up to it. Bob, can you try CPR?" Sam asked, her heart pounding as she ran up the stairs and followed her partner into the bedroom. "I'm going to put the phone on speaker. We'll try between us."

Bob removed his suit jacket and got down on his knees. Sam did the same on the other side of Bert Wade. One look at him, and Sam could tell it was too late. She glanced up at Iris who was fearfully hugging her daughter.

"Please help him if you can," Iris said before she broke down.

Jessica moved her mother to the other side of the room and settled her on the bed, their backs facing them.

Sam stared at Bob. "Let's see what we can do, partner."

The operator went through the technique that could possibly save Bert Wade's life. Sam and Bob were still at it ten minutes later when the paramedics arrived at the house. The older of the two men requested Bob to move back, and he took over. After a few minutes, he glanced up at his partner and shook his head.

"Sorry, he's gone."

Iris screamed and then broke down in her daughter's arms. Sam stared at the pair of them, glued to the spot, unable to function properly until Bob dug her in the ribs with his elbow.

"Are you okay?" he whispered, close to her ear.

Sam felt dazed and confused. Bob took over dealing with the paramedics and then whisked Sam down the stairs and out the front door.

She sucked in a few lungfuls of fresh air and stared off into the distance. "My God, how can this be? He seemed to be okay until Jessica turned up."

"Really? That's hardly fair. You might want to keep those kinds of thoughts to yourself, boss."

"Why? It's the truth. I wasn't saying anything that you probably haven't thought yourself."

"That's beside the point. It's not something that should have been said aloud at a time such as this, though."

He was right. She was in the wrong even suggesting it in the first place. She gave her head a good shake to rid herself of the offensive thought. "I'll give you that one, you're right."

"Hey, I know I am. We can't hang around here all day, Sam."

"I know. We'd come across as heartless if we leave now, though."

"Leave it with me. I'll get us out of here and save face at the same time."

Sam smiled. "I'll be taking notes."

He went back into the house and reappeared not long after with a large grin. "All done, we're free to go. I'll tell you all about it in the car."

Sam frowned, and he winked. They made their way back to the vehicle and got in.

She glanced back at the house to see one of the paramedics collecting a trolley from the back of the ambulance. "I don't envy them. What did you say to the family?"

Bob snapped his seat belt in place. "I told them a member of the team had been in touch with a possible lead we needed to follow up on."

"And they fell for it?"

"We're on our way, aren't we?"

Sam tapped her fingers on the steering wheel. "I hate the thought of lying to them at a time like this."

"We couldn't have stayed there, Sam. You know as well as I do what would have been likely to happen if we had."

Sam started the engine and drove off, then said, "We would have been forced into taking them to the hospital and wasting valuable time."

"You've hit the nail on the head. It's been a time-sucker of a morning as it is. We wouldn't be doing the family any favours if we hung around, would we?"

"You're right... for a change. Let's get back to the station, get the investigation started in earnest. There's nothing more we can do for them here." Sam's mind wandered back to Iris and how she would cope. "I fear for Iris. I know it's wrong of us to become emotionally involved with a family. But damn, hasn't that poor woman suffered enough today as it is, without dealing with the death of her husband as well?"

Bob sighed. "There's nothing we can do about that now, is there? All we can do is go back to the station and get our heads down, get the investigation solved as soon as is humanly possible."

He was right, for the third time that morning. Wonders would never cease to amaze her.

CHAPTER 3

When they arrived back at the station and filled in the rest of the team on what had taken place at the parents' house that morning, a gloomy cloud descended that was hard to shift for the rest of the day. Despite the team having good news for Sam upon their return.

In their absence, they had managed to locate the bike, or what they presumed was the bike, on one of the cameras relatively close to the Wades' house at nine-thirty on Saturday evening.

"This is great news. What about the plate, have you run that yet?"

Oliver nodded. "Nothing coming back so far, boss. I've researched how many bikes of that type are in the area, and we're looking at hundreds within a twenty-mile radius."

Sam inclined her head. "That doesn't seem too bad to me, Oliver, what am I missing here?"

"I'm not sure. I've got a niggling seed of doubt going on."

"Let's hear it."

"The fact that the killer used the bike and didn't bother

disguising his numberplate. Why would he do that and risk getting caught?"

"True, but if this is the only lead we have to go on, we have a duty to chase it up."

"Oh, I am, boss. Sorry, I shouldn't have spoken out of turn."

Sighing, Sam ran a hand down his arm. "No, I shouldn't have snapped. It's been a bad day so far. We're all doing our utmost for the family, I appreciate that."

"I'll keep searching, go through the camera footage, see if I can clock the bike on the way to the house."

"Good idea. I'll leave that in your capable hands, Oliver." Sam moved around the room with her coffee in hand. She came to a standstill next to Alex. "How's it going, old-timer?"

He chortled. "I can still give these young 'uns a run for their money, boss."

"I'm sure you can. Any news on the gas canister for me?"

"I've been in contact with a couple of ex-army mates. Apparently, a few months ago there was a cache of weapons seized that had been imported into the country illegally."

"Do they know where from?"

"Poland, they think. The information was a bit sketchy at best."

"Can you keep digging? Ask around, maybe get in touch with some dealers who sell this kind of stuff? Is it on sale on the open market?"

"I doubt it. Let me keep working on it for a day or so. Hopefully I'll come up with the goods soon."

Sam squeezed his shoulder. "Thanks, let's keep on top of this angle, Alex. It's an integral part of the crime."

"I'm aware of that, boss."

Sam winked and said, "I know I can count on you to get the job done, and swiftly, Alex."

"You can."

She continued making her way around the room and paused to chat with Claire, who was focussed intensely on her computer screen. She jumped when she realised Sam was peering over her shoulder.

"Crikey, my heart almost came to an abrupt stop."

"Sorry, I was keen to see what was holding your interest so much."

"I've got a few tabs open. One is regarding the husband's and wife's bank accounts. Nothing of relevance there, not really, unless you count a sizeable lump sum of twenty thousand transferred from John to Fiona in twenty twenty."

"Hmm... okay, that might have been when she started up her boutique business. John's mother told me that he funded the opening."

"That would make sense. Apart from that, there's the odd five hundred or a thousand transferred from John to Fiona. There's a transaction for five thousand to Thomas Cook. I'm presuming it was a deposit for a luxury holiday back at the end of last year."

"Okay. Fiona was diagnosed with breast cancer at the beginning of the year and went through treatment for months. Maybe that's when they had an inkling something was wrong and decided to jump on a plane and forget about their problems, have some family time together for a week or so. Make a note of it. I'll run it past his mother or John himself, if he wakes up. I'm hoping against hope he does that soon, the questions are mounting up. Questions that by the sounds of it, only he'll be able to answer. Any news on the business front?"

"I checked with Companies House. The business has been in his name for the last fifteen years."

"Only his name, or have there been other directors or partners involved in that time?"

"Only John Wade's name."

"And have we got a clear insight into what kind of business the company conducts?"

"Exports worldwide. It doesn't go into specific detail. I suppose we could try and obtain a court order for the company's accounts."

Sam thought over the proposition, and her nod increased in tempo while she contemplated the suggestion. "Yes, that's a good call. Let's get the ball rolling on that, Claire. We might as well, if John is as bad as we think he is. The sooner we get our hands on the accounts the better. Who knows what we're likely to stumble across?"

"My thoughts exactly, boss. I'll get on the blower now, get it actioned ASAP."

Sam made a beeline for her office and went over her notes. It had been a productive day but also a super frustrating one as well, to be expected with three murders and a victim's life on the brink. After a few minutes, she set the notes aside and dealt with a couple of urgent emails that had arrived during her absence and, before she knew it, Bob was knocking on her door, telling her it was almost seven and reminding her at the same time that they had skipped lunch during the day.

"Damn, it never even crossed my mind." With that, her stomach grumbled painfully. "Ouch, you should have said something sooner."

Bob shrugged. "Ordinarily, I would have done. To be honest, it even slipped my mind, too caught up in proceedings today."

"Sorry, Bob. I made a promise to you a few months ago that I wouldn't allow it to happen again, and here I am, breaking my word."

He wagged a finger. "Nonsense, if I was that bothered about filling my stomach, I would have shouted up earlier. Let's put it down to one of those days and forget about it."

"If you insist. I still feel gutted about it. Are you off now?"

"Do you mind? I promised Abigail and Milly I would take them out for a meal at that new Indian restaurant in town as an early treat for Milly's birthday."

"How wonderful. You go. I have a bit more paperwork to deal with before I head home. Have a good evening, send them both my love, and I'll see you in the morning."

"If you're sure? I don't mind postponing for a day or two."

"You might not mind, but trust me, the two ladies in your life will be absolutely livid."

He cringed. "Yeah, I think you know them much better than I do sometimes."

"It's a female trait, not wanting to have a promise broken."

"Okay, I'll take your word for it. I'll check in with you in an hour. By that time, you should be at home with your feet up, right?"

"I will be, you have my word. Now go. Tell the others I said thanks for all the effort they've put in today but now it's time to bugger off home."

"Or words to that effect, eh?" He chuckled.

Sam smiled and got back to work, resolute about finishing what lay ahead of her and being home by eight at the latest. She'd give Rhys a call from the car on the way.

As predicted, Sam hitched on her jacket at seven forty-five. She'd called Doreen, her neighbour and dog sitter, to warn her that she would be late home that evening. As usual, Doreen had told her not to worry and that Sonny was fine where he was, tired out from chasing the ball in the garden at regular intervals during the day. She rang Rhys.

"Hi, it's me. Sorry I'm late, I'm on my way back to the house now. Where are you?"

"Just pulled up outside the cottage. Do you want me to

collect Sonny and take him to the park? I could do with clearing my head," Rhys replied.

"You spoil us both rotten. I'd love to take him but I'm that weary, I don't think I have it in me this evening. What shall we do for dinner?"

"I know we're trying to cut back on the number of takeaways we eat, but shall we take the plunge this evening? Sounds like you've had a shocker of a day as well."

"I have, and why not? I could make a slight detour on the way. What do you fancy?"

"You decide. Get two of our favourite dishes, and we'll share."

"That's a deal. I'll see you in about thirty minutes." Sam indicated and pulled over. She scrolled through her phone for the takeaway's number and placed the order just to save her having to wait longer in the shop. Job done, she continued on her journey and was sitting outside the Chinese ten minutes later. She locked up the car and slipped inside the shop.

The petite woman with the beaming smile greeted her with a bow of her head and gestured for her to take a seat. She switched on the TV for Sam while she waited for her order to arrive. The local news was on and, as expected, the major headline consisted of the case Sam was dealing with. She found the utter tripe the journalist was spilling to the audience quite interesting, and Sam presumed it mainly comprised of hearsay the woman had gathered from the neighbours. Not once had the journalist tried to contact her for a comment before going on the air. That type of nonsense and bad manners got Sam's back up more than anything else she had to deal with in her career. She'd always considered she'd had a good rapport with the journalists in the area, giving them what they wanted in return for only putting facts out to the public, but this woman was new. Sam hadn't had the privilege of dealing with her in the past.

She made a note to track the journalist down the following day, to point out the error of her ways and the inaccuracies she had revealed.

"Such a shame." The lady behind the counter shook her head. "Poor family decimated like that. Never expected to see that type of thing when we moved here twenty years ago."

Sam agreed. "Thankfully, these sorts of crimes are few and far between."

"Oh, I don't know, it seems to happen regularly now, far more than it did when we arrived here. It's a big concern for me."

"Concern? Are you contemplating going back home? I thought you were settled here."

"Oh, I am, mostly. But who wants to live on the edge every day of their life? It's hard running a business like this. Sometimes I fear for my life. Maybe a chancer will come in here one day and rob me, that's always at the back of my mind."

Smiling, Sam handed the woman one of her business cards. "And if that ever happens, I want you to give me a call right away."

"Oh gosh, I never knew. All this time you been coming here to see us and I had no idea you worked for the police. I sorry, my husband always telling me I let my big mouth run away from me some days."

"There's no need to apologise, all you were doing was sharing your concerns, you have a right to do that. My team are working on this investigation, you really shouldn't believe everything you hear on the news."

"Ah, hubby tell me the same. I'm the type who thinks people have a responsibility to share accurate details. Are you telling me she's wrong?"

"Yes, we haven't given a public statement yet. Until we do, this journalist has chosen to divulge what she's learnt from people like you, the general public, and neighbours of the family involved, which is riddled with inaccuracies."

"Oh no, that terrible," she said in her cute Asian accent that was easy on the ear.

A man of a similar age opened the door behind the counter and handed her a paper carrier bag. "It ready," he said and smiled at Sam. "You enjoy. It made with love and care."

"I'm sure. If I didn't enjoy your food, Mr Wong, I wouldn't keep coming back for more."

He bowed, smiled and disappeared again.

His wife giggled. "You make his day."

"I'm glad. Only telling him the truth. Thank you. I'd better get home now, it's been a long day."

"Good to see you again. You have a pleasant evening and enjoy your meal."

"Thank you, see you again soon."

SAM WAVED AT DOREEN, who was looking out for her to come home. Her neighbour left her viewing spot and rushed to the front door. "How are you, Sam?"

"Tired. So sorry to impose on you today."

"Don't be. You know how much I adore Sonny, it's always an honour to look after him. You work too hard, isn't it time you had a break? You need a holiday to recharge your batteries, we all do from time to time."

"Rhys and I have been discussing hiring a camper van and taking off down to Devon or somewhere like that, in the next month or so."

"And why not? You deserve time off, you have a heavy schedule. I've just been looking at the news. Don't tell me you're involved in that murder case I've been hearing about?"

"All right, I won't, but I am. Don't listen to the woman on the news, she gave out a lot of misinformation that I will be pulling her up about tomorrow."

"That's terrible, how irresponsible of her."

Sam shrugged. "It's what we have to deal with now and again." Out of the corner of her eye she saw Sonny come bounding towards her. She bent down to make a fuss of him. He whimpered and jumped up at her. "Hello, sweetie, have you missed me?"

Sonny's whimpering increased.

Rhys joined them with Casper who was straining on his leash to get to her. She crouched and allowed the pup to place his paws on her lap. "Not forgetting you, too, sweetheart. Have you had a good day with Daddy?"

"He's been a pain in the rear for most of it, keen on disrupting the sessions I had this afternoon. I think boredom is setting in."

"The offer is always there for me to care for him as well, Rhys," Doreen volunteered.

He smiled at their neighbour. "You're a treasure, but I fear he would test you to your limits, Doreen."

"Oh well, maybe when he's a bit older, it's no bother. Anyway, I'll let you get on with your evening. It's late enough as it is, and I can see you've brought dinner home with you."

Sam pecked her on the cheek. "Thanks, Doreen. See you in the morning."

"I'll look forward to it, Sam."

Rhys opened the front door to the cottage, and they all piled into the hallway. Sam and Rhys removed their shoes and hung up the dogs' leads on the hook beside the coats.

"Do you think I upset her?" he asked.

"Who? Doreen? Why would you think that?"

They walked through to the kitchen, and Sam collected a couple of plates from the cupboard above the worktop while Rhys fed and watered their treasured pooches to prevent any likely begging at the table, which the ever-lovable Casper had resorted to in the past week or so, much to Sam's annoyance.

"Turning her down? It wasn't that the offer wasn't appreciated, but I don't think she realises just how much hard work puppies are. I'd forgotten. I love him dearly, but I have to admit that he drove me bonkers at times during the day. Luckily, most of my clients gain some benefit from stroking him during their visits, not all of them but most of them."

"It's true what they say then, about how much stroking a dog can lower your blood pressure," she replied.

"There's some justification in that assumption, yes. Enough about how tough our days have been, how are you in yourself?" He slid his arms around her waist and held her tightly.

"I'll be better once I've eaten. We forgot to stop for lunch today."

He pulled away, and Sam struggled to tell if she'd offended him or not. He opened the drawer to remove the cutlery they needed and laid the table.

Sam dished up, the hunger pangs in full flow now that she'd laid eyes on the food and the aroma had filled the kitchen. She deposited the plates on the table and sat opposite him. "Are you okay?" She had a feeling that she'd upset him in some way.

"Fine. I'm sorry you've had a rough day. Do you want to talk about it?"

She took a mouthful of egg fried rice and sighed. "Not really. This is a welcome treat. Dig in."

He seemed to hesitate before finally picking up his fork and diving in. Once he started, he continued without coming up for air.

The conversation ended between them right there. Sam didn't think anything of it until Rhys rose from the table and cleared away the plates and threw the cartons in the bin.

"Are you okay with me?" she asked, placing her head on his back and sliding her arms around his waist, mimicking what he'd done to her before they'd eaten.

He twisted so that he was facing her and put a finger under her chin, forcing her to look at him. "Why shouldn't I be okay with you? Stop searching for things that aren't there, Sam. I'm not Chris, I would never treat you the way he did, so stop worrying."

She smiled. "Hey, I know that. You went quiet on me, that's all, and I thought I had offended you."

"Not in the slightest, nor would you, ever."

"You can't be sure about that. Let's make a drink and see what's on the TV."

"Do we have to? I'd rather sit and chat, or have a cuddle with you, either is fine by me."

Sam kissed him on the cheek and slipped out of his embrace. She collected two glasses from the cupboard and withdrew a half-finished bottle of wine from the fridge. "What are we waiting for? I can't even be bothered getting changed tonight."

"That makes two of us."

They openly discussed how their day had panned out. Rhys insisted Sam should go first. He was always interested in hearing about the investigations she worked on, and she was equally keen to hear about what he'd been up to with his clients most days.

"Hey, talking of which, one of the witnesses, I'd say the main witness so far, has agoraphobia, and I gave her one of your cards."

"That was kind of you. Will she be able to come to the office?"

"I don't think so. I said that you might go and visit her at home. It's a lovely place, one of the new-builds out in Stainburn."

"I think I know the ones. That's okay, no problem for me to go and see her. Is she going to give me a call?"

"I hope so. I've laid the groundwork. You can't lead a horse to water, though, can you?"

"You're right, you can't. Is she quite bad?"

"I'd say so, yes. Will you take her on if she calls you?"

"I've yet to turn down a person who chooses to seek out my help, Sam."

"Good. She seems a nice lady. She tends to spend all of her time nosing out of the front window. It's such a shame there are people out there who are crying out for help but who are afraid to seek advice."

"Every individual is different. Some are eager to get help whereas others get stuck in a routine and find it impossible to break it."

"I got the impression she was fed up being a slave to her condition."

"Then we'll have to see if she calls me. Come here." He slung an arm around her shoulder and pulled her close to him.

Sonny jumped up on the sofa behind her, and Casper sat on the floor in his soft bed at their feet and was asleep within minutes.

"Poor boy, he's worn out," Sam said.

"Don't feel sorry for the menace, and I'm not surprised he's tuckered out, he's had me in and out of the office all day long. I must have walked him around the block a dozen times or more."

Sam laughed. "The joys of having a pup."

"Yes, mistake number one. Maybe I should have taken a trip down to the rescue centre instead."

Sam sat upright and stared at him, open-mouthed. "You don't mean that?" she asked eventually.

"Don't I?" He untangled himself from her grasp and left the room.

Sam stared at poor Casper, curled up in his bed, oblivious to what was going on around him and the trouble he had caused during the day. She went in search of Rhys and found him in the kitchen, leaning against the doorframe of the back door which was open.

"Hi, are you okay? You didn't mean it, did you?"

Rhys took a while to answer. "Didn't I? Let's just say he's not Benji."

She took a step closer. "No, he's not, no dog will ever be able to replace Benji." Guilt bit her in the arse. *I'm not going there. I said I would never raise the subject again.* When her ex-husband had chosen to take his own life, right outside their cottage, he'd taken Benji with him and driven Rhys out of her life for a few months.

"I know it's wrong of me to expect so much from the little one. I thought I was up to the challenge when I brought him home. I guess I forgot how much hard work it is to have a pup to care for."

She placed a finger under his chin and forced him to look at her. "It's not his fault. He's a baby. An adorable one at that. He'll come good with your love, guidance and training, I have no doubt about it."

He moved his head out of her grasp and stared at her. "You reckon?"

"Totally. He's a babe in arms, all legs and lacking in brains at present, but I'm sure he'll come good, given half a chance. Please don't give up on him."

"I won't, not intentionally. Maybe this is all down to my ignorance. Forgetting how time-consuming they can be at the best of times."

"That's just it. People who buy puppies have to make the effort to mould their babies, otherwise it's just not going to work, is it?"

"Don't I know it? The problem is, Benji was such an all-round good dog..." His voice drifted off, and he glanced at the sky.

Sam hugged him. "I know, but you're forgetting all the hours of training you had to put in at the very beginning."

Reluctantly, he hugged her back. "I know I'm probably being irrational. Let's put it down to having one of those days and getting maudlin about the past."

"We all have them. Why don't we plan a week's holiday, hire the camper van like we said and do some intensive training with Casper while we're away?"

"Do you think I'm asking too much of the little fella?"

Sam smiled and pecked him on the cheek. "Possibly. It's a tough call taking a pup to work with you and expecting it to behave all day at that age."

"What's the alternative?"

"Fit in more break times? I know that isn't always easy with your hectic schedule."

"It's not. Okay, I'll see what I can do. Thanks, Sam."

"For what? I didn't do anything."

"For being supportive and not shaming me into feeling guilty."

"Never. We all have our problems, some easier than others, for someone else to solve with well-meaning advice. I'm always here for you, with an open mind and heart, if ever you need to chat. Casper will come good in the end, with patience and love to guide him."

"Let's hope so. Do you want another drink?"

Sam's mobile rang on the kitchen counter. "Why not? I'll need to get that, Bob said he would check up on me."

"He's a good man."

"He is that." She left his embrace and answered the phone. "Hi, yes, I'm at home."

"Good to hear it. How are you doing?"

"I'm stuffed, full of a Chinese from Mr Wong's."

"I need to give that place a try, you've mentioned it a few times." He lowered his voice to add, "The Indian meal out was a non-starter, don't ask, so we settled on boring old cottage pie and runner beans instead."

She resisted the urge to giggle. "I'm sure Abigail made it with a lot of love and attention and it was super tasty."

"Hmm… if you say so. What's on the agenda for you tonight?"

"Nothing much. Chilling with a glass of wine and doing some training with Casper."

"Puppies are hard work, but the effort will be worth it in the end. Did you catch the news earlier?"

"I did. Stupid bloody journalist. I've made a note to ring her in the morning."

"A case of a newbie trying to impress her boss, right?"

"Possibly. She's not going to know what's hit her when I deal with her tomorrow. I was going to tell you to remind me but I don't think you're going to need to. I'm that bloody wound up about it. Anyway, my glass of wine needs my full attention now. Have a good one, Bob."

"You, too, Sam. See you in the morning. All right if I sit in while you tear the journo to shreds?"

"Feel free." She laughed and ended the call.

Rhys topped up her glass and handed it to her. "Did I miss something?"

Sam cast her mind back to the timings of the evening. "You were probably at the park with the dogs. While I was waiting to pick the food up, Mrs Wong turned on the TV to keep me entertained. There was a journalist spouting all sorts of nonsense about the investigation we started this morning."

"Heck. She obviously hasn't heard who's in charge of the case, God help her."

Sam swiped him across the arm. "Cheeky sod. You'll regret saying that, mark my words."

"Now I'm scared. Want to take this upstairs, so you can punish me for speaking out of turn?"

She laughed. "Why not? We can come down later to let the dogs out."

CHAPTER 4

Watching and waiting were his best assets at the moment. He'd pulled up outside the house he had been staking out for the third time in as many days, making notes about the family's routine. He knew the time to attack would be that evening, all his preparations in place. Time was marching on. He glanced over his shoulder, aware his bike was out in the open, as he'd planned all along. Not bothered in the slightest if he was caught out on one of his scouting missions or at the crime scene itself. He had nothing to live for, so what the heck did he care?

He hopped off the bike and undid the strap holding his bag in place on the shelf behind the seat. It had several weapons inside, intended to do more harm than good. He slid down the side of the house and entered the back gate, aware that the family were in the lounge as he'd seen them fighting over the best seats in the house for their viewing delights. The wide-screen TV had sprung to life, and he recognised the film they were watching, one of the *Star Wars* movies, although he had trouble recalling which one.

Something made him pause. The main man, the husband,

was moving around in the kitchen. He ducked behind the trunk of a large leafy tree close to the fence and watched Cole Thompson leave the house and start up his BMW, parked in the space at the rear, and drive off.

Shit, where is he going? His mind raced at a hundred miles an hour. *Do I call off the attack this evening? Or sit and wait for him to return? Shit! I'm torn between a rock and a hard place. I need this to happen tonight, it has to!*

Sod it, he was still going to make his move. He left his hiding place and approached the back door to the detached house, which Cole had thoughtlessly left unlocked. He paused, surveying the area behind him. It was an open garden, lots of flower beds and a specific play area over to the right for the children which included a trampoline built into the ground. The kids were all around the same age. The eldest girl was thirteen or thereabouts, then there was another daughter, slightly younger, and a boy who was the baby of the pack—he guessed him to be around ten. He hesitated for a moment as memories of his own children entered his mind. He shook his head, ridding himself of the laughter and happier days that had filled his distant past. That's all they were now, memories. He had nothing left. Nothing, all because of...

He didn't have time to linger in the past, not now. The time for reflection would come later, once he'd successfully carried out his lethal mission. His heart rhythmically pounding against his ribs, he carefully pushed open the back door and entered the house. Envy struck him as soon as he stepped into the kitchen. State-of-the-art equipment littered the worktops.

And yet, I bet they're never used, not if they go out for takeaways all the time. How the other half live when they have money burning a hole in their pockets. I have a job to do, now, stop thinking of what might have been and get on with the task in hand.

He crept through the kitchen and into the hallway. The noise of the film worked in his favour, covering any possible squeak the floorboards might make that could alert the family of his presence.

After reaching the lounge, he placed his bag on the floor and dipped his hand inside, locating the kitchen knife. He removed it and teased the edge of the blade with the tip of his gloved finger. *Hello, my beauty, it's time to go to work.* Next, he pulled a balaclava from the bag and pulled it over his face. He was ready to rock and roll now, and the family wouldn't know what had hit them. The door swung open, and four stunned faces turned his way. The mother opened her mouth to scream.

"You do that, and I will kill your children, make them suffer one by one as punishment."

Her mouth closed but dropped open again to ask, "What do you want from us?"

He chose to ignore her. "Where's Cole?"

"He's... he's gone to pick up dinner, from the Indian down the road, he should be back soon. Why are you doing this?"

Again, he refused to answer. "Shut up, your inept questions won't get answered."

"What do you want?" Danielle asked again, her voice trembling with fear.

The boy was sitting on the floor by his mother's feet. He could see the defiance in his young features but chose to ignore it. The two girls hugged each other, and the older girl reached out to hold her mother's hand.

"Isn't this nice, all of you playing happy families like this? It's wonderful to be surrounded by your loved ones, isn't it?"

"Yes, we're very close," Danielle agreed. "Please, if you're after money, we don't keep any in the house, the risk is too great."

"I'm not. I'm seeking revenge."

Danielle's brow pinched into a deep frown. "Revenge for what? We haven't done anything to you, have we?"

"Oh yes, plenty. I've been working up to this, preparing for the right time to come and pay you a visit, and that time is *tonight*."

Danielle gulped. "What do you mean? How has my family wronged you?"

"I've said enough." Extending his arm, he waved the knife back and forth, his intentions clear.

Suddenly, and before his mother could stop him, the boy ran at him and yelled, "Leave my mother and sisters alone. Come on, big man, I'll take you on."

He suppressed a giggle and held out his other arm which connected with the top of the boy's head, preventing him from getting any closer. "You calling me big man, when you are acting like this. You think you can take me on, boy?"

He lowered his hand, and the boy surged forward. Rory aimed his head at his gut; it didn't connect because the knife slit the boy's throat before he could get any closer.

Danielle and her two daughters screamed, the girls covering their eyes.

"No, you can't do this. Why did you hurt my baby?" Tears mixed with snot ran down Danielle's face.

He leered at her. "Because... I can. He was stupid to take me on. You'd be wise not to try to do the same, you hear me?"

Danielle nodded, and she poked her daughters to do the same. "You have our word."

He pointed the bloody knife at them. "Don't move." He clawed around the lounge door for his bag and removed the pieces of rope he'd cut into medium-length strips.

"Hey, you." He pointed at the youngest daughter.

Her head swiftly turned to face her mother.

"Don't look at her, come here. Don't be scared."

Danielle nodded. "Do as he says, Kaitlin. Please, don't hurt her," she pleaded, the tears still flowing from the devastating loss of her son.

"If she does as she's told then she will remain unharmed. If she doesn't, she'll end up like her brother, the choice is hers."

"Mummy, I don't want to go to him, I'm scar... ed," Kaitlin whispered, her body quivering as fear took hold.

"Come, I won't hurt you, little one," he said, his voice light and friendly.

"Go, Kaitlin. You'll be safe."

Danielle's gaze latched on to his, pleading with him not to rob her of yet another one of her children.

He lowered the knife, true to his word, giving the impression that he wouldn't hurt the child. When Kaitlin finally plucked up the courage to leave her seat and walk towards him, he saw the terror set deep in her bright-blue eyes. He held out the pieces of rope, and her shaking hand grabbed them.

"Take them back and give them to your mother."

She backed up, keeping her eye on him all the way to her seat.

"What do you want me to do with them?" Danielle asked.

"Tie your daughters' hands and then loop one piece around your own wrists, I will finish it off."

Danielle heaved out a sigh and kissed her children on the cheeks. "Forgive me, Hannah and Kaitlin."

"It's okay, Mummy," Kaitlin said. She climbed back onto the sofa to snuggle up next to her sister.

"Don't do it, Mum. Don't listen to him. He's going to kill us. He didn't think twice about killing Rory. What makes you think he's going to stop there? He hasn't told you what he wants with us yet. This could be a trick. Don't fall for it,

Mum. Dad will be back soon, don't do anything rash, let Dad deal with him when he gets back."

"Quiet, Hannah. Don't antagonise him. Just do as you're told, for me, for us."

"I refuse to." Hannah sat on her hands in an attempt to prevent her mother tying them together.

"Impertinent children should not be tolerated. In my country, she would be sent away from home to obtain a certain degree of manners, working for another family, begging for her food every night."

"That would never happen in this country. Please forgive her, she's terrified. This isn't her speaking, it's the fear."

"You don't have to speak for me, Mum, I'm able to do that for myself. I've been brought up to know right from wrong. He's in the wrong. Why are you allowing him to dictate to you?"

"Because... he's already killed your brother!" Danielle's voice faltered on a sob. "I don't want to lose either of you. For me, Hannah, do it to appease your old mum."

Hannah closed her eyes and exhaled a large breath. "All right, I'm doing this for Rory."

"Good girl," Danielle said and wrapped the rope tightly around each of her daughters' hands then loosely tied the third piece of rope around her own wrists and tugged at the ends with her teeth to pull up the slack. "There, I'm secure, what now?"

He relaxed a little and stepped forward to complete the task. "I haven't decided yet."

He ran a finger down Danielle's cheek, and she turned away from him in disgust.

"Don't touch me, don't touch any of us. Cole will deal with you when he gets back."

"He must be a mighty brave man, your husband. Are you sure you know him as well as I do?"

Her brow furrowed. "What are you talking about? How do you know him?"

"That's my secret. I intend to keep it for a while, there is no need to share it with you. Before you *die*, I will tell you this, that your husband is not who you think he is."

"*Die*? You're going to kill us?" Danielle's gaze drifted to the pool of blood surrounding her son's lifeless body. "Why? Just give me a reason!"

"I have plenty of reasons, believe me. Your husband and his friend have done considerable damage to a lot of peoples' lives, and look around you, you've been reaping the rewards for years."

Danielle gasped. "You killed John's family, didn't you?"

"Yes, that's right. They deserved it, just like you do."

She shook her head. "No, I don't care what my husband is guilty of, what he does has nothing to do with me and the children. You can't punish us for his misdemeanours."

"That's one word for what he's been up to, not something I would ever use to describe the carnage he has caused."

"Carnage? What the hell are you talking about? You have to tell me. Maybe I can make amends in some small way. If you want cash, we could come to some arrangement. I don't have money here but I can get hold of some. Name your price."

He leaned in and through gritted teeth said, "You sound desperate. No amount of money will right the wrongs he has committed against me and my people, you hear me?"

"I hear you but I don't understand what you mean."

"You think you know what your husband gets up to? You don't, that much is obvious. Unless you are trying to trick me into believing you are innocent in all of this."

"All of what? I am innocent. I have no idea what you're talking about."

He knew this woman was lying to his face, and his temper

rose. He slapped her. Her head snapped to the side, and a bone clicked in her neck.

She cried out. "What the hell was that for? You have to believe me. I'm telling you the truth. Whatever your gripe is with my husband, it's him you should be dealing with, not subjecting me and my family to this... whatever this is. You're a despicable coward, that's what you are. You were obviously waiting outside, hoping my husband would leave before you entered the house and started all of this. How could you? What sort of man kills an innocent boy for challenging him?"

"Granted, I should have kept him alive. I sense he's more of a man than his own father is."

"Why are you saying all of this? Tell me what Cole is supposed to have done to you. How do you know him? Through his work?"

"You ask a lot of questions for someone in such a precarious position. Why?"

"You've already told me that you intend to kill us, the least you can do is tell me why."

Hannah and Kaitlin began crying, and Danielle tried to comfort them, but it was difficult with her hands tied.

"Hush now, girls, let Mummy try and get to the bottom of this, bear with me."

"Mummy, he's going to kill us, like he did Rory. What's the use?" Hannah pleaded with her mother, her voice breaking on yet another sob.

"Ssh, baby. Leave this to me. Be brave, both of you. Mummy will get us out of this."

He laughed. "If that's what you believe then you are as idiotic as that husband of yours." He glanced up and caught sight of the black BMW returning, and panic rose within. He kicked himself for not getting the job done properly in Cole's absence. He raised the knife again and completed the job he'd come here to do, making sure all the screams were constrained before Cole got out of his vehicle. Then he left the room, took up his position in the cubby hole under the stairs and waited.

Whistling coming from the kitchen confirmed that Cole had entered the house. He left it a few moments, aware that the man had been out for food and was probably busy dishing up the meals. Movement, footsteps in the hallway. He prepared himself for the surprise he had in store for the man of the house, his hand ready to push open the cubby hole door and jump out at him as he passed.

"Jesus, what the fuck is this? Who are you?" Cole dropped the two plates of food he was holding and covered his heart with his hand then took a couple of steps backwards.

"I'm your worst nightmare, come to haunt your dreams for the rest of your life, you miserable fucking bastard."

Cole frowned. "Yeah, bring it on. You don't scare me."

He could tell the man was talking bullshit, he was agitated. His gaze drifting behind him, over his shoulder at the lounge and his hands clenching and unclenching by his side.

"Go on, I think you're anxious to see your family. Take a look. You'll find them where you left them, in the lounge."

Cole took a tentative step towards the lounge. The door was now closed, hiding the horrors beyond. Cole cautiously peered over his shoulder.

"Go on, I dare you," he challenged the man he'd grown to despise and distrust the most in the world.

Cole eased the lounge door open and poked his head into the room. He let out a frenzied yell and collapsed to his knees.

Coming up behind him, he lowered his head to Cole's and sneered, "Now you know what it feels like to have your whole family wiped out."

Cole clutched at the doorframe and clambered to his feet. "How could you do this to them, to me? Who are you?"

"I am the man who is going to beat you to within an inch of your life, so that you can relive this day, over and over in years to come."

The hammer came down on Cole's hands still resting on the doorframe and moved to his knees, four swift blows before Cole had the chance to fight back. Cole dropped to the floor and cried out, the pain evident in his features.

The blows kept coming, one after the other, until Cole's upper body sank to the floor.

He checked Cole's pulse, it was still quite strong, then he collected his bag and left the house, but not before he stabbed Cole in the stomach. On his way out, he intentionally left the back door and gate open so that the family would be found sooner rather than later. He wanted Cole to remain alive.

A neighbour passed him by in the alley. He'd removed his balaclava by then.

"I think someone needs help in there." He jabbed a thumb to the fence at the bottom of Cole's garden.

"Cole having trouble with the kids again, is he?" the neighbour asked jovially.

"Something like that," he shouted and broke into a run.

The bike roared into life, and he left the scene, a huge grin set in place as he weaved through the traffic on each side of the road, drawing attention to himself once more.

CHAPTER 5

Sam was mortified she received the call at ten that evening. She was having an after-sex cuddle with Rhys and groaned. "I'm sorry. I should get this."

"Be my guest. I've had my piece of you this evening, the rest can have their share now."

She pinched his cheek. "You really do say the most romantic things. I can see why I hooked up with you now." She swiftly answered the phone before he could shoot back a witty retort. "Hi, DI Sam Cobbs, how can I help?"

"Sorry for the late call, ma'am, it's the control room. I've been asked to contact you by Professor Markham. He's attending a murder scene at present and felt you should be informed rather than call anyone else at the station."

"Fair enough. I take it he wants me to attend the scene also?"

"Yes, that was the idea. Sorry if I didn't make myself clear."

"It's late, I'm not about to pick apart your choice of words, not at this time of night."

"I appreciate that, ma'am. These twelve-hour shifts take

their toll on you now and again. Thanks for being so understanding," the female operator said.

"You'd better tell me where I need to go."

"It's twenty-eight Turnpike Road in Branthwaite."

"Can you brief me on what to expect?"

"Professor Markham insisted he should be the one to fill you in, ma'am."

"Okay, not to worry. I should be there within twenty minutes. Can you do me a favour and contact my partner, DS Bob Jones, and request his attendance? I'm warning you, he won't be happy."

"Don't worry, thanks for the heads-up. I have broad shoulders. I'll give him a call now."

"Thanks." Sam hung up and turned to see a dejected-looking Rhys eyeing her. "You got the gist of that, I take it?"

"Hard to say no when you've been summoned, eh?"

"If the pathologist has requested my company, it usually only means one thing." Sam put on fresh underwear but chose to wear the suit she'd worn for work during the day. She turned to see Rhys frowning.

"Meaning?"

"That he believes there's a possible link to a case that's already on the go."

"Damn, I hadn't thought of that."

"Do you want me to put the dogs out when I go downstairs?"

"No, you shoot off, I'll see to them."

Sam finished dressing, combed her hair in the bathroom and quickly brushed her teeth, aware how keen Markham was at picking fault with her choice of food, especially when she'd eaten anything garlicky. "I'm fit to go. Sorry for running out on you like this. Hopefully I won't be out long. That's the plan, but then I always say that."

"You do what you have to do, Sam. Just stay safe out there. I'd tell you to ring me when you get a chance, but yeah, don't bother, not at this time of the night. Is that selfish of me?"

"Utterly, but also totally acceptable." She brushed her lips against his, tempted to stay in that position longer. She finally pulled herself away from him and got her journey underway.

Bob called her when he was en route. "How long before you get there?" he asked.

She could tell he was pissed off, it was evident in his voice. "Another five minutes, according to the satnav. What about you?"

"About the same, six if you want to split hairs, not that I would dream of being so cantankerous, especially at this time of night."

"No, of course you wouldn't. I'm tired, I need to give my driving my full attention, so I'm going to hang up now."

"See you soon. Drive safely."

"That's the intention, I assure you."

She turned the radio up in an attempt to keep herself alert. Five minutes later, Sam drew up alongside Des Markham's pathology van. Bob arrived not long after. She removed two suits from her boot, avoiding another telling-off from Des about equipment not being handed out willy-nilly at a crime scene.

"Are you ready for this?" Bob asked. He fastened his suit and snapped on a pair of gloves.

After completing her ensemble in record time, Sam nodded. "Let's do this. Front or back?"

Bob thumbed over his shoulder to the rear of the property. "I'm guessing we should go round the back, there seems to be more activity going on around there."

"Maybe we'll get home before midnight."

"What will happen if we don't? Will you turn into a pumpkin?" Bob sniggered.

"I have no idea in your case."

"Charming. I needn't have come out this evening, in fact, for a quieter life, maybe I shouldn't have."

"From me?"

"Nope, Abigail. She gave me the evils when I walked out the door, we were about to… I shouldn't need to fill in the blanks, when I received the call."

"A definite mood killer, right?"

"Were you still up?"

"No, but I won't go there. I couldn't handle your envy."

"Eww… too much information. I hope you had a shower before getting on the road?"

Her cheeks heated up under his intense stare. "Let's call a halt to this conversation while I still have an ounce of dignity left."

He laughed, and they made their way down the alley and into the back garden. The gate was open but cordoned off with crime scene tape. Sam and Bob signed the log, and the officer on duty lifted the tape for her and Bob to duck under.

Des Markham appeared in the doorway and welcomed them with one of his awkward smiles. "Ah, you've finally made it. All suited up, I see. Don't forget to cover your boots before you enter the house."

Sam waved her booties at him. "Wouldn't dream of it. How many dead?"

"Three kids and an adult. The husband was whisked off to hospital before I arrived, so I only have hearsay about his injuries."

"Shit! Same MO as the last one?"

"Same as the last one, where all the family was killed bar the father, which is the reason behind me requesting your company. I hope you didn't mind, tough if you did," he added with a smirk.

"We didn't mind, did we, Sergeant?"

"Not in the slightest, boss," Bob agreed, rolling his eyes at Sam when Des turned away from them.

"Good, good. Let's get cracking then, shall we? I'll walk you through the crime scene, once you're fully protected."

Sam and Bob took the hint and slipped their booties over their shoes and then followed Des through the back door and into the vast kitchen.

"Jesus, this room is huge, double the size of mine, not that I'm jealous or anything," Sam stated.

"Yes, yes, can we get on?" Des tore through the kitchen, his suit rustling noisily in the unnerving silence of the house.

They entered the hallway and were confronted by a large pool of blood and food spillage from what appeared to be two broken plates.

"This is where the husband was found. I've been told that he suffered from a knife wound to the stomach. There were also patches of blood on his knees, either from further injuries or maybe he crawled through his own blood. Actually, forget that, there would be smears and not pools of blood, if that were the case."

Sam eagerly surveyed the area and spotted the blood on the doorframe. "Did he try to get off his knees and use the doorframe as an aid to assist him?"

Des seemed puzzled by the question. "Possibly. I'm thinking along the lines that maybe his hands were injured in situ, but what do I know?"

"You mentioned his knees being injured but not his hands."

"As I've already said, his injuries are hearsay, and I'd rather not comment on something I haven't seen with my own eyes. You should know how I work by now, Inspector."

"Oh, I do, believe me. I was guilty of thinking out loud, so feel free to ignore me."

"Whatever. Please be careful as you enter the lounge." Des swivelled on his heel and went into the room.

Sam frowned at her partner.

He shrugged and said, "I guess all will be revealed soon."

She thought she'd prepared herself enough for what lay ahead of her, but when she saw the massacre for herself, she had trouble keeping her Chinese down. "Jesus Christ! What the fuck is wrong with this person? Two families eradicated, or as near as, dammit, in the same week. Why?"

"There's really no point in you asking me that, not at this stage, Inspector," Des shot back at her abruptly.

"It was an observation which ended with a rhetorical question, Des."

"Ah, okay. Just putting you straight before you go down that dubious route. Want to hear what I think?"

"I'm all ears. I'm struggling to work out what happened here myself."

"Not sure if you spotted it, but there's food in the kitchen and on the hallway floor, plus takeaway cartons. My assumption is that the father nipped out to collect it, possibly took the boy with him—that part I'm unsure about—leaving the wife and the two girls at home, watching the TV."

Sam assessed the position the bodies were in. "Okay, sounds plausible to me, except the father is outside the room and the boy is a few feet inside. Are you suggesting he came rushing in here and the killer slit his throat, was more than likely awaiting his arrival? Were the mother and daughters killed before or after the lad lost his life? Because there seems to be something off about that evaluation."

"I agree. To me, the way the boy is lying, I would have put him in the room with the others." Bob demonstrated what he thought happened next. "What if he was sitting on the couch with the others, the killer entered the room, and he jumped out of the chair to defend his family? With his father out of the picture, he would most likely have wanted to do that, seeing himself as the man of the house at the time."

Des took up his thinker pose. "Possibly. You think he went on the attack and the killer cut him down, literally?"

"Unless anyone else has a better idea. Putting myself in his shoes, it's what I would have done to protect my loved ones. It wouldn't have mattered if I was the youngest in the room or not."

"I think that's very perceptive of you, Sergeant. Sadly, I have no way of confirming if that is the way things occurred or not."

"It was worth a shot, something to consider. It all boils down to the same thing. Someone entered the house and slaughtered this family," Bob said.

"They did," Sam said. "Any sign of forced entry, Des?"

"Nothing as yet. Maybe the husband nipped out and left the back door open and the killer seized the opportunity to come in that way, in his absence."

Sam's gaze shifted from the child lying a few feet inside the door to the mother and her two daughters. Each of them had stab wounds to the chest and additional wounds to the throat, just like the boy. "Overkill?"

"What gives you that idea?" Des asked with a touch of sarcasm.

"The double wounds. Can I get closer to them?"

"Sure. Just be careful of the markers on the floor."

Sam smiled and nodded. She stepped around a few patches of blood staining the cream-coloured pile carpet and stood in front of the mother and daughters. "They've been bound, but the boy wasn't."

Bob joined her to assess the victims' positions. "Which kind of backs up my idea of the boy leaping to his feet to defend his family. Maybe the killer slaughtered the boy then tied up the rest of them before they could attempt more of the same."

"He's good," Des said from behind them. "It does seem to be a logical conclusion. Well done."

"Yes, well done, partner," Sam said. "All we need to determine now is in what order these three were killed."

Des shuffled forward, avoiding a marker on his immediate right. He raised a hand and brought it down on the woman's chest, then did the same with the older daughter, and finally, the younger child. "Maybe the killer stabbed them first then decided that the boy had bled out quickly from his wound and thought he'd ensure the females would die swiftly by slitting their throats, too."

Sam inhaled and exhaled a breath as she imagined the terror the family must have been subjected to before their deaths. "Horrendous. Who called nine-nine-nine, do you know?"

"Yes, the neighbour next door. And yes, maybe I should have told you something earlier."

Sam rolled her eyes. "Go on, surprise me."

"The neighbour thinks he may have spoken to the killer."

Sam spun around and faced him, almost toppling over in her haste. "You what?"

"Yes, my apologies. He passed him in the alley. He was coming home from work, I believe. I switched off after that, you know what I'm like about treading all over someone else's role at a crime scene when I have enough on my plate already."

"Jesus, Des, yes, you should have told me about this the second we arrived. Come on, Bob, we need to get around there. Which neighbour?" she asked, conscious about keeping her temper in check and not really succeeding, judging by the shock on Des's face.

"On the right. I'm not going to keep apologising, Inspector. I've been up to my neck in it since I arrived."

"It's forgotten. We're off. We'll call back in to see you before we head off."

"You do that," Des shouted after her. He swore under his breath, probably realising his mistake, not that he tended to make that many.

She was prepared to forgive and forget, this time.

"What a plonker," Bob said on their way out of the back door.

They removed their protective suits and accessories and popped them in the awaiting black sack, and then Sam shifted up a gear and marched next door. The neighbour was waiting for them, standing guard at the window in the kitchen. Sam waved as she entered the garden. Solar lights lit up the path to the back door. He opened it.

She dug in her pocket and withdrew her warrant card. "Hello, sir. I'm DI Sam Cobbs, and this is my partner, DS Bob Jones. We've been told that you called nine-nine-nine, is that correct?"

"Yes, do you want to come in? I'm Graham Bell by the way. I don't think I gave my name to the official-looking man I spoke to earlier."

"That would be Professor Markham, the pathologist. Thanks, sorry to show up so late, we've not long been notified ourselves."

"It's okay. I'm not an early-to-bed type of person. I doubt if I'll be able to sleep tonight as it is."

Understandable, in the circumstances. There had been nights at the beginning of her career when sleep had evaded her, too. Not so much these days, now that she was hardened to all the vicious crimes she had to deal with.

Graham motioned for them to join him at the table. He picked up a glass, half-filled with amber liquid, and took a large gulp. "Sorry, can I get you a drink? Not one of these, not with you being on duty. A tea or coffee perhaps?"

"A coffee would be great. Why don't we let my partner make it while you and I have a quick chat?"

"Yes, I'm up for that. The cups are on the side, the cutlery just below and the caddies are over to the left. You'll find some milk, not much, in the fridge. I've got UHT I can use if you run out."

"I'll make it stretch, thanks," Bob replied and headed over to the counter to fill the kettle.

Sam noted the man nervously turning his crystal glass on the coaster. "I'm sure it must have been a shock to find the family like that this evening. Can you tell me what happened?"

"I was late coming home from work. I met a guy in the alley; he seemed in a rush. He mentioned that Cole 'needed help in there'. I made a joke and asked if he was having problems with the kids again. He grinned and said, 'something like that'. He didn't hang around. I heard a motorbike start up a few seconds later. The back gate was open. Cole and I are good friends. I also noticed the back door was open. I stepped into the kitchen and called out. I saw the takeaway bag on the worktop, presumed they were having their food so left them to it." He shook his head. "Why in God's name did I do that?"

"Please, don't go blaming yourself."

"I'm not, not really. I just wish I hadn't given up and come home, I should have persevered. My stomach was grumbling, not having eaten all day, and the thought of tucking in to the wife's chilli was too much of a draw for me."

"Don't worry about it. So you had your meal and then went back to check on the family?"

"Yes, around half an hour later. I thought it was strange that the back door was still wide open. Something didn't sit right with me. My stomach was tied up in knots as I entered the house. I called out again—I don't make a habit of barging into Cole's house uninvited. When there was no answer, worry took over, and I ventured into the hallway, and that's when I saw him, lying there in a pool of blood. How I held on to my stomach contents, I will never know. I've completed a first-aid course at work and checked for a pulse. It was not how it should be, I suppose you'd call it relatively weak. Not surprising, the amount of blood he'd lost. I decided to call nine-nine-nine and ask for the ambulance to attend. They got the police involved as well. I stayed with Cole, never thought about looking in the lounge for the others. It seems nuts now that I think about it, considering the injuries he had suffered." His hand slid through his greying hair. "Why didn't I check on Danielle and the poor kids? Why?"

Sam placed a hand over his. "It's not your fault. Is your wife around?"

"No, I sent Marie off to her mother's, she was terribly upset. I didn't think either of us would get any sleep tonight with all this going on. She's got an exam at work in the morning, for a possible promotion. I didn't want all of this to affect her and for her to screw up."

"It's okay, don't fret about it. When did you notice the rest of the family?"

"Not until I heard the sirens in the distance. I spent most of my time checking Cole's pulse et cetera and stemming the bleeding, like the operator instructed. What a bloody nightmare this is. To have your family killed in a blink of an eye. He's going to be traumatised when he wakes up, if he wakes up."

"Do you know which hospital he went to?"

"Whitehaven. They reckon he should be awake by the morning. I dread to think how he's going to take this news."

"It's best not to think about it. We'll ensure someone is

there for him when he wakes up."

"How can anyone think about wiping out a family like this? Kill that beautiful woman and the children? They were such good kids, maybe a little spoilt, but nothing over the top."

"Can you tell me more about the man you saw?"

He puffed out his cheeks and closed his eyes. "I'm trying to visualise him now. He spoke with a slight accent."

Bob joined them and fished his notebook out of his pocket and jotted down the details.

"As in a regional accent or a foreign one?"

"Definitely foreign. Lord knows where from, though, sorry, I'm crap with things like that."

"His height and build?"

"He was around six feet, maybe a couple of inches taller. He had a slight beard, not a goatee, but a full one that was just sprouting, if you get my drift?"

"I do. This is excellent. His clothes?"

"Jeans and a black leather jacket, or did he have black leather trousers on? I'm not sure, it was one or the other."

"You said you heard a bike. A large one or a type of moped?"

"No, a heavy-duty one. He revved it loudly before he drove off as if making the most of the moment."

"Did you see the bike?"

"No, sorry, only heard the roar of the engine."

"Are there any cameras on this road? In either Cole's home or yours perhaps?"

"No." His answer came swiftly, but then his brow wrinkled. "Wait, I think Ken told me the other day that he'd installed one of those cameras at his front door. Yes, he did, plus he mentioned that he'd bought a dashcam at the end of last year. Whether that works when the engine is switched off, well, that's a different story."

"Any idea, Bob?"

"I can do some research. Last I heard the car had to be running, but maybe they've come up with new technology recently."

"Can you do a search for me now?"

Bob withdrew his phone and began the search. "Yeah, as I predicted, if the camera is linked to the cigarette lighter, depending how old the car is, it'll switch off when the car engine dies. However, here's an interesting fact, there are some car models that if you set them to parking mode the camera will continue to record."

"Ah, that makes sense. I suppose we need to find out what type of camera your mate has got installed, Graham."

"Do you want me to give him a call?"

Sam smiled. "It's not too late for him?"

"No, he'll be fine. We often have a natter at this time of night if we see each other's lights on." He picked up his mobile and pressed a number which connected soon after. "Hey, Ken, yeah, it's me... I've got them with me now... they've asked me about cameras on the street, and yours came to mind. Yeah, sorry if I've dropped you in it... Great, the lady in charge seems really nice... You would? That would be fantastic. Come round the back, mate." Graham placed the phone on the kitchen table and sat back. "He's going to pop over and see you, you know, that way you'll be able to kill two birds with one stone, won't you?"

"That's very thoughtful of you and will save us going over there after we've finished here."

A knock sounded on the back door, and it opened. "Hi, I'm Ken. What's going on next door, mate?"

"Crap, sorry, I should have made you aware over the phone." Turning to face Sam, he asked, "Is it okay if I tell him?"

"If you want to."

"Take a seat. As you can probably tell by all the vehicles outside Cole's house tonight, it's not good news."

Ken pulled out a chair next to Sam and said, "I came home late. Susie had an evening appointment at the hospital, don't ask. I think the strikes aren't helping and have screwed up their schedules. I wanted to see her settled in bed first before I rang you to see what the gossip was. So, what happened?"

"I found Cole in the hallway, he was unconscious. He'd been attacked, but that's not the worst part. All his family has been killed. Butchered, they were. It's like something out of a horror movie." Graham's head bowed, and he twisted his glass on the coaster.

"You what? Butchered? Are you telling me they're *all* dead?"

"Yep, Danielle and the three kids have been taken from us."

"How? Who did it, do you know?" Ken directed his question at Sam.

"Unfortunately, we don't, not yet."

"That's where you come into the equation, Ken." Graham glanced up again, his eyes swimming with tears.

"Me? What? I didn't have anything to do with this, how could you think such a thing?"

Sam shook her head. "No, you've got the wrong end of the stick, that's not what Graham was suggesting."

Ken slammed back in his chair. "Thank fuck for that. Damn, sorry about the language, but Cole is a friend and good neighbour to all of us. Everyone on the close will tell you the same. This isn't making any sense to me. How did he survive and the others haven't?"

"Exactly. We believe it was intentional," Sam replied. She sighed and revealed the truth, believing Cole's friends deserved to know what they were dealing with. "I have to tell you this is the second case of this nature we're investigating this week."

"What?" the two men said in unison.

"That's right. They're both very similar. The other man was also left alive, he's in a very bad state. I'm not saying that Cole's injuries aren't significant in the slightest, however, it would appear, by what the pathologist has told us, that they're not as life-threatening as the first victim's."

"He was stabbed in the stomach, that's how I found him. Plus, his hands and knees were all smashed up. I reckon some fucker took a hammer to him," Graham filled in.

"Seriously?" Ken asked. "Why? Why would someone do this to Cole?"

"That's what we need to find out," Sam said. "Graham told us that you'd recently had cameras fitted in your car and at home, is that correct?"

"Yes. What are you asking? If my cameras picked up anything tonight?"

Sam smiled and nodded. She crossed her fingers. "We're hoping that's the case, yes."

"Well, me being out this evening at the hospital isn't going to help you because the car wasn't in its usual position, so we can dismiss that. But…" He withdrew his phone and punched in his passcode, then flicked through the screen. He tapped his finger and said, "I've got an app that I use for the door camera."

Sam glanced at Bob and raised an eyebrow then she turned her attention back to Ken again. "Here's hoping you can help. What we're specifically looking for is the killer's getaway vehicle, which Graham believes was a motorbike."

"I'll see what I can do. Any idea what time I should be aiming for?"

"The bloke passed me at around seven-thirty."

Ken's head jutted forward. "You saw this guy? The killer?"

Graham gulped. "Don't make me feel worse than I already do. I did, he was in a rush and spoke to me. I'm presuming he took off on a motorbike as I heard one start up moments after he went out of view. I, um… I didn't discover Cole until around an hour later. I called out when I found the back door open but I saw the takeaway bag on the worktop and presumed they were eating and didn't want to be disturbed, so I popped back after I'd had my dinner. Only to find him lying there in a pool of blood. Thankfully, he was still alive. The paramedics who attended told me not to feel bad because I'd probably saved his life calling them when I did, but I still feel bad, so much time lost, well, he might have died in that time, just like his family."

Sam patted Graham's arm. "Please, you need to stop blaming yourself. He's alive, let's cling on to that, for now."

Graham offered up a weak smile. "Yeah, okay, you're right, I suppose."

"Sorry you had to deal with this, Graham. Let's see what I can find on my camera."

They all fell silent, anticipation growing within Sam as he ran through the footage. Eventually, Ken punched the air and angled the phone towards Sam. Bob leaned over to view the footage at the same time. She saw a man dressed in leathers fasten a helmet in place, start up the bike, rev the engine a few times and put his foot down to leave the close.

"That's fantastic. Is there any way we can get a close-up of the numberplate?" Bob jumped in before Sam got the chance to ask.

"I'll have to try and play around with it. It's a new piece of kit, and I've yet to find out the ins and outs of how it works properly."

"I've got a better idea," Sam pitched in. "If you can share the footage with us, we can get the lab to do all we need and more."

Ken pulled a face. "Again, I'll have to check with the manual, if I can find it, to see how I download the footage. Can you leave it with me overnight and I'll get back to you in the morning?"

"Sounds great to me. Thanks for all your help, Ken."

"It's what friends do for one another, isn't it?"

"Cole will be devastated about his family when he wakes up," Graham added. "Poor bloke. I wouldn't want to be in his shoes, but we'll be there to see him through it, won't we, Ken?"

"Too right we will."

"Do you know if they have family in the area?"

The two neighbours glanced at each other, and Ken shook his head while Graham shrugged.

"I feel like we're letting you down," Graham said.

"You're not. You've both given us plenty to be going on with. We'll do the necessary digging at the station, unless you think any of the other neighbours might know?"

"I doubt it. Wait..." Ken peered up at the clock on the wall. "Susie might know. I could ring, see if she's gone to bed yet. Knowing her, she'll still be up watching TV."

"That would be super, if you wouldn't mind?"

Ken made the call. "Sorry, love, I hope you weren't asleep... I'm here over at Graham's, talking to the detectives in charge of the investigation. They've asked us if we know if either Cole or Danielle have got any family in the area. Neither of us can give a definitive answer. So I was wondering if you know... Ah, okay, it was worth a shot. I'll be home shortly... yes, everything is okay here. Don't worry, I'll fill you in later. Love you." He ended the call. "Christ, my heart was racing, that was tough. I didn't want to tell her over the phone. She's going to be distraught when she learns Danielle and the kids are gone."

"It doesn't seem possible, does it? You'd think you'd be

safe in your own home, wouldn't you?" Graham asked.

"It's always better to keep all your doors locked and add extra security these days," Sam suggested. "Have either of you seen anyone hanging around the close lately? Maybe spotted the bike around before?"

"No, nothing is coming to mind," Graham replied. "Ken?"

"No, I can't say I've bothered looking out for anyone, well, you wouldn't, would you? Not until something like this happens. I'll be getting extra cameras installed and an alarm system now, that's for sure."

"Okay, if there's nothing else you can tell us, then we'll get out of your hair. I'll send a uniformed officer around to see you in the next day or so, Graham, to take down a statement."

"I'm in and out, it might be better if I came to the station," Graham said.

"Either way is fine by me. Thanks again for all you did tonight, Graham. I'm sure Cole wouldn't still be with us if you hadn't stepped in to help out."

"I don't know about that. I hope he makes it. Will it be okay if we visit him?"

"Yes, we'll have an officer on guard outside his room, but I'll be sure to inform them that you intend to drop by for a visit." Sam stood and held out her hand to shake Graham's. "Thanks again." She then shook Ken's. "And if you can get that footage over to me ASAP, I'd appreciate it. I'll give you both a card, it's got my phone number and email address on it, in case you need it."

Ken took the card. "I'll try and find the manual tonight, and sort it for you, Inspector."

"Thanks, I know you'll do your best for us, and for Cole."

Sam and Bob left the two men sitting in the kitchen and exited the house via the back door.

"Another bloody tough case has fallen into our laps," Bob

muttered.

"I'd rather deal with this than let someone else come along and screw it up."

They walked to the end of the alley, and Sam surveyed the area.

"There aren't that many lights on around here, therefore, I don't feel inclined to start knocking on doors, pissing people off for waking them up."

"What are you saying? That we call it a night?"

"Not yet. I think we should go back to Cole's house, see what we can find. We'll need to get suited and booted again first."

"Great, and there was me getting my hopes up that this was going to be a quick one tonight."

"You would have got that at home, had you stuck around."

Sam left him standing there, his mouth gaping, and went to retrieve the protective gear from the back of the car. Once Bob had recovered from his slap in the face, he reluctantly joined her.

"I'm saying nothing," he grumbled.

They re-entered the house and visited the lounge first to check in with Des.

"How's it going?" Sam asked.

"Ask me in a couple of hours."

"That bad, eh? Any clues yet?"

"Not yet. We're still working through the scene, taking lots of photos and examining the blood spatter for now. That's going to keep us going long into the early hours of tomorrow morning. How did you get on?"

"We've got some footage of the killer leaving the scene on a motorbike. The image is going to need enhancing at the lab. The guy is going to get the footage to me in the morning, if he can figure out how to download it. It's late, I'm not sure he was thinking straight."

"New-fangled technical devices are the bee's knees if they come with easy instructions. If they don't, then most people are up shit creek. Let me know when you send it in and I'll ensure you're looked after."

"Thanks, I was hoping you'd be able to give them a friendly nudge."

"Or a kick up the arse if they slacken off, you mean."

Sam grinned at him. "Is it all right if we have a nose around? I asked the neighbours if the family had any relatives in the area, but neither of them could give me a definitive answer."

"Yes, you go ahead. The relatives should definitely hear about this, and soon. Are you aware that a TV news crew are hanging around out there? I caught sight of the woman when I was retrieving some equipment from the back of the van."

"Shit, no, we came straight here." Sam kicked herself for not seeing the van when she surveyed the area. She peered out of the small side window, and there she was, the journalist Sam was intending to call first thing in the morning.

Damn, I can't waste another suit. She's bound to still be out there when we've finished. I'll deal with her then.

"I can see her, lingering with intent. I'll have a word with her after we've had a look around, if that's all right with you, Des?"

"Do what you like, just keep out of my way, as usual."

"Of course. Bob, let's start in here by checking the sideboard. You take that side. We're searching for an address book."

"Doh! I figured as much," Bob replied sarcastically.

Sam groaned. "Behave. If you want to get home sometime tonight, you'll cut the crap."

"Get you."

They searched the drawers on either side of the middle cupboard in the piece of furniture but drew a blank.

"Nothing at all." Sam clicked her fingers. "Des, have your guys seen a mobile lying around, close to either the husband or the wife?"

Des got up off his knees and crossed the room to where all the evidence bags had been laid out. "Is this what you're looking for?" He held up a plastic Ziplock, and inside it was a pink iPhone.

"Perfect, let's hope it's unlocked."

Des tutted. "Yeah, right, in your dreams. If it's the wife's, I bet it's locked, especially with nosey kids hanging around."

"Fair point. I'll give it a shot anyway." Sam switched the phone on but, as suspected, it was locked. "Another job for the lab to deal with."

"I'll ensure they get on it in the morning."

"We're going to have a nose around upstairs."

Bob followed Sam out of the lounge, and they ascended the stairs together, but split up at the top.

"It might be worth searching the kids' rooms, they might have the grandparents' numbers written down somewhere in case of emergencies," Bob suggested.

"Good call. I'll search the main bedroom while you make a start on the kiddies' rooms." Sam travelled the length of the hallway and walked into the largest bedroom, assuming that to be the master. A king-size bed dominated the room, and there was a bank of built-in oak wardrobes along the length of the far wall, opposite the bay window which overlooked the close. Sam couldn't help herself, she crossed the room and sought out the journalist pacing the end of the close. Her temper rose and heated up her cheeks. She was going to have pleasure dealing with that bitch once they had completed the job in hand. "First things first, let's see what I can find around here."

She drifted over to the other side of the room and opened the wardrobes. Her immediate thought when she saw the contents was that there were no men's clothes anywhere to be seen.

"How strange." Sam went to the door and peered down the hallway, counting the number of doors. There were six. Assuming one of them belonged to the main bathroom that meant this was a five-bedroom house. If the three kids had a room of their own, that left one spare room. She took a punt and poked her head round the door on the other side of the landing. There was a double bed in there with en suite facilities. Sam opened the wardrobe door and saw men's suits and shirts hanging on the rails.

Bingo. I think they were sleeping apart, or possibly going through a separation. The plot thickens.

She came out of the spare bedroom and went back into the master to begin her search. Bob joined her around five minutes later.

"Anything?" she asked.

"Nothing, just lots of toys in the boy's bedroom and about a thousand quid's worth of make-up in both the girls' rooms, as per usual."

"You men, always bloody exaggerating where women's spending is concerned."

He pulled a face and wobbled his head at her.

Sam ignored his annoying mannerisms and plodded on. "This looks promising." She extracted a pink notebook from the drawer of one of the bedside tables and waved it in Bob's face.

"You won't know unless you open it and have a butcher's."

Sam riffled through the pages and found Danielle's mother's number under the M tab. "Here's her number. No address, though, not even her name."

"Bugger, that's going to be a difficult call to make. Considering the company we have outside, no matter what time of night it is, I think you should give the mother a call this evening. We could both pop round there and see her to break the news."

"I was thinking along the same line." Sam inhaled and exhaled a couple of large breaths to prepare herself. "It's ringing," she whispered.

The phone rang four times before a sleepy woman's voice answered, "Hello, do you realise what time of the night it is? Who is this?"

"I'm so sorry to disturb you. Umm… would I be speaking to Danielle Thompson's mother?" Sam glanced up to see her partner squeeze his eyes shut, cringing in despair.

"Yes. Why?" There was a slight pause before the woman gasped. "Oh my, who is this? Has something happened to my daughter?"

"I'm sorry, I should have introduced myself sooner, I didn't want to scare you. I'm DI Sam Cobbs of the Cumbria Constabulary."

"And? I asked you a question. Is my daughter okay?"

"Would it be possible to come over and see you?"

"I'm not liking the sound of this at all. Is she all right? Yes or no?"

"Please, Mrs…?"

"Parker, Brenda Parker. If you're avoiding the question then she's clearly not okay. Tell me!" She ended her sentence by screaming at Sam.

The scream sent shockwaves rippling through Sam's taut body. "I'd rather not tell you over the phone. If you give me your address, I'll come and see you now."

"It's ten Wishburn Road, Lillyhall. Do you know it?"

"Not personally, but I'm sure the satnav will be able to track you down. We'll be another ten minutes or so here." Sam squirmed, knowing that she'd given too much away uttering those few words. Even if the woman was drowsy from being woken up, she still clearly had her wits about her.

"Here? Are you at my daughter's house?"

"Yes. We won't be long, I promise."

The call was ended by Brenda Parker.

"Shit, shit, shit!"

"Hey, you had to contact her. It was obvious you calling at this time of night that the news wouldn't be good. Don't go blaming yourself, Sam, there was no way around this."

Sighing, Sam nodded. "I know, but it's still upsetting, being aware that I've destroyed someone's world and I haven't even broken the news properly yet, if you get what I mean?"

"I do. Don't think about it. Is there anything else we need to do here?"

"I don't think so. Wait, I need to show you something major that I discovered."

"Intriguing. What's that?"

She took him over to the wardrobes and asked for his observations on the contents.

"Another woman with too many clothes to her name, what's different about that?"

"You don't get it, do you? There's no men's gear in there."

He faced her and frowned. "So?"

She hooked her arm through his and pulled him across the hallway. "Now what do you see?"

"Another room with a double bed in it."

"Go and open the wardrobe."

"Bloody hell, it would be a lot simpler and less time-consuming if you'd just come out and tell me what's on your mind," he said, disgruntled.

"It's called testing your observational skills," she insisted.

"It's called winding a cranky, tired copper up at eleven-thirty in the evening."

"All right, you win. All his clothes are in here."

"So, what does that prove? She's got a shopful of clothes

in the main bedroom which leaves him using the spare room to store his gear. I bet that's the same story in dozens of households throughout the UK. What are you getting at?"

"That they were probably separated."

"If you say so, then it must be right. Me, I'm inclined to believe my assumption outtrumps yours. I guess we'll find out soon enough when we have a chat with the mother."

"Yeah, another reason why I'm not looking forward to speaking with her. Come on, I still have that clown outside to tackle before we deal with that particular task."

"Oh, what joy! And there was me thinking this night couldn't get any worse. Lead the way, Mistress of the Night."

Sam tried not to laugh but failed and swiped him. "What the fuck? That name brings to mind so many different connotations, all of them *bad*."

"Does it?" he asked in all innocence.

Sam remained unconvinced and turned on her heel and left the room. She stopped briefly in the lounge to say farewell to Des and then, with the bit between her teeth, she exited the house, discarded her protective suit, gloves and booties and deposited them in the black sack, then made her way around the corner to the journalist.

"You might want to curb that temper of yours, I can tell it's on the rise," Bob said from two paces behind her.

"I'll handle her how I deem fit, but thanks for the advice."

"Don't mention it. It's me who has to bloody deal with the consequences, so all I was doing was trying to make my life easier. Worth a punt."

Choosing to ignore his well-meaning advice, she approached the journalist, who was practising what she was about to say on live TV, and tapped her on the shoulder. The young woman with vivid green eyes spun around to confront Sam.

"Do you mind? Unless you have something valuable to

say, I suggest you go back to your home and let the professionals deal with this," the spunky young woman spat at her.

"And what is *this*?"

"*This* is going to be a live broadcast for the local news, going out on the air at just after midnight. Now, if you'll excuse me, I have preparations to make."

"Well, *this* professional is about to come down heavily on you."

The journalist's gaze ran the length of Sam's body from the top of her head to the tips of her leather ankle boots. "Excuse me? You're a professional, in what respect?"

There was something about the way she was trying to sum Sam up that really pissed her off. Sam dug into her pocket and pulled out her warrant card. "Don't push me, lady. I'm DI Sam Cobbs, the SIO on this investigation."

The colour rose in the journalist's cheeks but subsided again just as quickly. "Ah, now we're talking. I was going to give you a call in the near future."

"You were? And I was going to do the same in the morning. I guess I needn't bother now. What's your name?"

"Colleen Brass."

"Well, Colleen Brass, what I want to know is where you're getting your information from."

"My what?"

"Your information. Look around you. It can't have gone unnoticed that you're the only journalist out here at this time of night. Why do you suppose that is?"

Colleen had the grace to appear embarrassed, if only fleetingly. "We're keen to get to where the action is, always have been. Where better than to report from the actual crime scene? Is there a law against that, Inspector?"

She had Sam over a barrel, there wasn't, not as such. "You know the answer to that as well as I do, Miss Brass. What I'm getting at is, why you always seem to be first to a crime scene, in particular, two that have occurred this week."

"What can I tell you? I've got a nose for sniffing out good stories. While you're here, why don't I interview you about what's gone on here tonight?"

Sam shook her head. "Don't push your luck. I have work to do. You'd be advised not to reveal any of the details you've uncovered so far this evening."

"May I ask why? No, wait, you haven't told the family yet, have you?"

"That's correct. We're on our way over there now. I'd rather they heard the shocking news from this *professional* as opposed to hearing it from the likes of you."

"Ooo, are you allowed to make such bitchy comments, Inspector Cribbs?"

The defiance grew in Brass's eyes, and the fact that she had got Sam's surname wrong, obviously on purpose, wound Sam up.

"If you think that was bitchy, stick around, lady."

Brass grinned, her perfect, pearly-white teeth glistening in the glow from the streetlight a few feet away. "Hey, that's my intention, for the next few hours at least. If there's a story to be had, I'll be there."

"And it doesn't matter a jot if you trample over a crime scene or the relatives' feelings, to get it, does it?"

"Nope, you're bang on there. So why don't you bow to the pressure and let me interview you, now, while you're not doing anything?"

Sam's blood boiled.

Bob could tell how irate she was becoming and stepped closer to the journalist. "You'd be wise to back off, Miss, if you know what's good for you."

"Ooo... the gorilla has a voice. How cool."

Bob's chest puffed out, and Sam latched on to his arm

before he could say or do anything else.

"Leave it, Sergeant, she's not worth it."

"Oh, I am, I assure you, Inspector. I'm climbing the ladder of success very quickly. You'd be wise not to forget that when making threats in the future."

"If you think I've threatened you in any shape or form, Miss Brass, then you really don't know me at all."

"I hear you have a reputation for shooting journalists down in flames. Well, I have news for you: that kind of behaviour doesn't wash with me."

"Thanks for the warning, and here's one for you. While we're having this friendly little chat, if you're going to go to air to report a crime, you'd be wise not to fill your reports with dozens of inaccuracies, like you did the other day."

"And they were?" Colleen inclined her head and smiled.

Sam wagged a finger. "You'd have to get out of bed super early to catch me out with that one, Miss Brass."

"It was worth a try. I report the facts as I see them. If the truth gets embellished slightly along the way, then so be it. Feel free to put me right if I overstep the line, won't you?"

"Willingly. Goodnight, Miss Brass."

"Good luck with telling the victim's family, Inspector Gibbs."

Sam glared at her and walked back towards her car.

"Effing cheeky bitch. We can do without her sort hanging around a crime scene, making our lives a misery," Bob murmured.

"You said it. Maybe we're dealing with yet another new breed of journalists, partner. We'll keep an eye on her. I won't think twice about tearing her to shreds if she reports the slightest inaccuracy in the future."

Bob chuckled. "I bet. Are we taking both cars?"

"It makes sense. We'll visit Danielle's mother and then head home, leave everything else until the morning."

CHAPTER 6

The semi-detached house was in a cul-de-sac close to one of the new housing estates. Mrs Parker had all the lights on downstairs and was at the front door to greet them when they drew up. Sam swallowed down the acid burning her throat and approached the woman with Bob joining her at the gate to the small front garden.

"Good luck, I'm right behind you," he muttered.

"Gee, thanks. I think it's going to be a traumatic half an hour or more." Sam removed her ID from her pocket and showed it to Mrs Parker. "I'm DI Sam Cobbs, and this is my partner, DS Bob Jones."

"You can call me Brenda. My husband, Ian, will be down soon. He's getting dressed. As you can tell, I didn't bother." She gathered her dressing gown at the collar as her husband came running down the stairs in black jeans and a bright-orange T-shirt.

"What's this about, and why wouldn't you tell my wife over the phone?" Ian Parker demanded before Sam had a chance to say hello to him.

"Is there somewhere we can have a chat?"

"Yes, let's go through to the kitchen. Do you want a drink?"

"No, we're fine, thank you."

Sam and Bob followed the husband and wife into a snug kitchen at the rear. The units seemed relatively new. At the end of the narrow room was a breakfast table, that's where they all settled down to hold their conversation. Mr and Mrs Parker held hands and pushed their chairs close together to accept the news Sam had hinted about on the phone.

"You were right, the news isn't the best that I could be sharing at this time of night. Earlier, we were asked to attend an incident at your daughter and son-in-law's home." Sam noticed the couple's grip tighten.

"Go on," Ian urged.

Sam swallowed. "When we arrived, your son-in-law, Cole, had been taken to the hospital."

"Oh God, is he all right?" Brenda asked.

"I don't know. I've decided to let him rest tonight and check in with him at the hospital in the morning."

"And our daughter and grandchildren?" Ian was the first to ask.

Sam's gaze dropped to her clenched hands for the briefest of moments as she prepared the sentence that was about to tear this couple's lives apart. Her gaze rose, and she did her best to blink back the tears misting her eyes. "I'm sorry, they didn't survive."

Brenda screamed. Her husband wrapped his arms around her and hugged her tightly. Brenda beat her fists against his back, but neither of them spoke for a few minutes. Sam and Bob sat still. The atmosphere was now fraught and sombre, which Sam thought was totally understandable and to be expected.

Eventually, Brenda pushed away from her husband and wiped her eyes on a tissue she pulled from a box in the centre of the table. "I'm sorry for breaking down. Danielle is, was, our only child. It's an impossible situation to deal with as I'm sure you'll appreciate."

"There's no need to apologise. I'm so sorry to be the bearer of such dreadful news. Take all the time you need to grieve. If you'd rather we left now and came back in the morning, that's fine with us, you only have to say."

"No, I won't be able to revisit this in the morning. I want to get it over and done with tonight. How did they... die?"

"We believe someone broke into their home, possibly while Cole was out, fetching a takeaway."

"Blast him, he should have been at home, protecting them. He and his damned takeaways. He's always been the same, putting his stomach before his family's safety," Ian went on the attack.

"Stop it, Ian. How is this his fault if he was out of the home when the intruder got in?" Brenda stated breathlessly.

"He probably left the damn door open, he's done it time and time again when we've called round there for a visit. People can't afford to do that these days. It's not like the old days when we all felt safe in our own homes. Too many bloody foreigners around, taking advantage of people's good nature. You'll know better than me about the statistics surrounding house burglaries, Inspector. I bet it has increased since the number of immigrants has gone through the roof in this country in recent years."

Sam shrugged. "I couldn't possibly comment, sir."

"Spoken as if you were a politician."

"Now, Ian, don't start antagonising the one person we need on our side," Brenda warned.

"I wasn't, not intentionally. Forgive me if it came across that way, Inspector. It's something I feel strongly about, and sometimes my mouth has a tendency to run away with me when I get worked up about the situation."

"There's no need to apologise, sir. We all have certain topics that make our blood pressure rise."

"You're not wrong. Has the culprit been caught? Who found Cole, if he's in a bad way?"

"One of their neighbours. He made the discovery, rang an ambulance and probably saved Cole's life. Sadly, he could do little about saving either your daughter or your grandchildren."

"Are you telling us they were already dead?"

"We believe so, at least that's the pathologist's initial assumption. We're going to need to speak to Cole before we can either confirm or deny that fact."

The couple clutched hands tighter, until the whites of their knuckles were on show.

"I just hope they went quickly," Brenda whispered.

"How were they killed?" Ian demanded.

Sam closed her eyes. It wasn't something she relished telling a grieving family, not on her first visit after a tragedy had occurred. "They had severe injuries that I believe would have taken their lives swiftly, if that's any consolation?"

"It isn't, but thank you for being open and honest with us," Ian replied.

Brenda sobbed some more and then asked, "Did they die together? Would they have seen each other die?"

"That's likely to be the case as your daughter and her children were found in the lounge. Are you up to answering any questions?"

"Questions? About the crime?" Ian asked.

"About their lives. For instance, have they mentioned recently if they've noticed anyone hanging around the house?"

The couple glanced at each other.

"Not to me. Has Danielle said anything to you, love?" Brenda asked her husband.

"Not a single word. Do you think this was a planned attack, is that what you're asking, Inspector?"

"I'm just asking the most obvious question, sir. When we were looking around the house, the bedrooms, I also noticed that Cole's clothes were stored in the spare room. Is there a reason for that?"

Brenda shook her head and sighed. "They were in the process of splitting up. They were trying to find the right time to tell the children. Cole made the decision to move into the spare room."

"That all makes sense now. May I ask why their marriage had ended or was in the process of ending?"

Brenda heaved out a shuddering breath. "Irreconcilable differences."

"Okay. Has your daughter sought out the advice of a solicitor?"

"Yes, Windsor and Bartlett's in Workington."

Sam nodded, and Bob wrote down the information in his notebook.

"I know it. How long has it been since your daughter initiated talks with the solicitor?"

"She visited Mr Wilson last month. All was going well, as far as we were led to believe. I don't think Cole was contesting the divorce at all, at least that's our understanding. Maybe the solicitor will be able to tell you more."

"I'll make a note to drop by and see him. I have to ask, was there anyone else involved?"

Brenda inclined her head. "Are you asking if either of them had an affair?"

"Yes, that's right. Did they?"

Again, the couple glanced at each other.

"Did she say anything to you, Ian?" Brenda asked.

"No, nothing at all. Our daughter wouldn't do that, she

thought too much about the children to put them through that kind of trauma," Ian declared.

"Yes, I agree. And I don't think Cole would do it either, he was far too busy at work."

"Where did he work?"

"He ran his own business. Well, he was a partner in a firm, has been for the past six months. Maybe that's when the cracks began to show in their marriage." Brenda nodded and added, "Yes, I think it was."

"What type of business?" Sam's interest notched up a level.

"An export business."

Sam's gaze drifted to her partner, and she waited for him to glance up from the notes he was taking. Eventually, his eyes widened when their gazes met, which didn't go unnoticed by the couple.

"What's going on? I know there's something you're not telling us," Ian demanded.

"Do you happen to know his partner's name?"

"It's John Wade," Brenda confirmed.

Sam inhaled a large breath. "Have you caught the news at all this week?"

"That's a strange question. No, we've been away for a few days, visiting friends. We only got back yesterday, and now this has happened, and I'm regretting going away and not spending time with our daughter. You never know when they'll be taken from you," Brenda said and broke down again.

Ian comforted her and kept one eye on Sam. She fidgeted under his glare.

"What are you trying to tell us, Inspector?" Ian finally got around to asking, once Brenda had settled down a little.

"Unfortunately, John's family was also attacked this week. He's the only family member to have survived. His life is hanging by a thread; he was transferred to Carlisle Hospital."

Brenda gasped and clutched her husband's hand. "What does this mean? That someone deliberately set out to hurt all of them due to the business?" Brenda asked.

Sam shrugged. "It's a possibility. We haven't got around to checking out the business side of things yet. We've been chasing our tails with the other investigation, trying to find family members to inform et cetera and doing the necessary background checks on the family. It only came to light during today that John Wade ran an export business. We were due to visit the office in the morning. Do they have other members of staff at the office who we can have a chat with, if we showed up there tomorrow? Any idea how large the workforce is?"

"There's a secretary, I think she's called Santy, but I'm not sure. I've spoken to her a couple of times when I've called to speak to Cole about making arrangements to help out with babysitting duties, you know, that sort of thing."

"Thanks. What about the rest of the workforce?"

Brenda paused to think. "They'd have to have some people, wouldn't they? You know, to load up the containers ready for exporting, that type of thing. Drivers to deliver the containers to the docks. Men at the warehouse to organise that side of things," Ian suggested.

"I would have thought so. Don't worry, we can do our research into the company in the morning."

"What about Cole, will we be able to see him?" Ian asked. "I mean, we'll want to get some answers from him, won't we?"

"The same as we will. Again, we'll call and see him first thing in the morning. He's been sedated this evening, which is probably a blessing in disguise, given what's happened to his family."

"Ha, if it turns out this has occurred because of that damn business of his, you'll need to restrain me when we do go and visit him," Ian said, his face contorting with anger.

"Now, Ian, that type of talk isn't going to help, is it?" Brenda said. "He's lost his family as well as us. We've got to stick together, grief will be consuming all of us. I don't want any extra unpleasantness at this stage, or in the future come to that. What's the point?"

"The point is, my love, that if he hadn't got involved in the business in the first place, our daughter and grandchildren would probably still be alive today. Someone has to pay for robbing us of our family, and in my opinion, that someone should be him."

Sam sighed. "While I agree with most of your statement, Mr Parker, until we do an in-depth investigation into the company, we really can't give a definitive answer about what's gone on there."

Ian released his grip on his wife's hand and left his chair. He paced the floor for a moment or two and then retook his seat. "Am I the only one who can see what's going on here?"

"Now, Ian, there's no need for you to take that tone, just calm down," his wife said. "It's late, the inspector is right, there's little she's going to be able to do at this time of night. Surely you understand that she will need to speak with Cole first, before she starts digging into the firm as such."

"Your wife is right, Mr Parker. As soon as I gather my team in the morning, we'll get to work on investigating the ins and outs of the company. Hopefully, Cole will also be able to shed some light on what this is all about."

"What about John? Is he going to pull through?" Brenda asked.

Sam raised her crossed fingers. "We need to remain positive. We're hoping to visit him in the next few days, once he's regained consciousness, but I think we'll need to put that on hold for now and concentrate on following up the leads we have for the new investigation."

"You mean finding out why our daughter and her three innocent children have been slaughtered," Ian said, irate.

Sam scratched her temple, the tiredness now beginning to affect her. "That's right, sir."

"And why can't you get on with things tonight?"

"Because we will need to gain the proper authorisation from the courts et cetera that will allow us to carry out the necessary searches at the business premises. Our hands are tied until we get those."

Brenda gathered her husband's hands in her own. "They wouldn't want to get started tonight, love, it makes sense to leave it until the morning when they have more manpower to deal with the investigation."

Ian placed his hands over his face and sat there for a while and then nodded. Appearing to be a lot calmer, he said, "Okay, you win. You need to find the person or people responsible for wiping out our family, Inspector. If you're not up to the task then I'll get out there and do it myself. And don't think that's a threat, it's a promise. I don't care if I end up in prison either, I need to get revenge for my family's deaths, and the only way I know how is to hunt this bastard down and string him up from the nearest bloody tree. What gives him or them the right to take one person's life, let alone four?"

"You're forgetting John's family in the body count," his wife reminded him.

"No, I'm not, that truly doesn't concern us. Yes, I feel sorry for his relatives, but our priority remains with our family, not someone else's."

"I hear what you're saying," Sam said, "and you have every right to feel angry about the situation, Mr Parker, but I assure you, this person will not go unpunished. My team have an excellent success rate, we won't let you down."

"I'm glad to hear it. Now, is there anything else? Because I need to spend some time with my wife, grieving our loss. We can't do that with a couple of strangers in our house, can we?"

Brenda looked shocked and then gave a brief nod. "He's right. We need to start the grieving process."

Sam agreed with the couple and stood. Bob followed suit. He flipped his notebook shut and slipped it into his pocket.

"Try to get some rest. I know that's going to be easier said than done."

"When will we be able to see them?" Ian's gaze bored into Sam's soul.

It was the one question she had been dreading either of them asking, given the extent of the victims' injuries. "Not for a few days yet. It's going to take time to complete all the post-mortems. I'll pass on your contact details to the pathologist. His department will be in touch when the necessary tests and examinations have been conducted."

"Thank you. Please, please, do your very best for us," Brenda pleaded, her hand clutched in prayer in front of her.

"I promise, we will give everything we've got to the investigation. Believe me when I say this, we want this person off the street as much as you do."

Ian got to his feet, ready to show them to the door. He walked the length of the room and said, "I doubt it. I'll show you out."

Sam and Bob both bid Mrs Parker farewell and joined her husband in the hallway.

"Don't kid a kidder, Inspector. What are the odds on you finding this vile person?"

"I'd say a hundred percent in our favour. Give us a chance

to get the ball rolling first, Mr Parker. We have no intention of letting you down, I swear."

"Make sure you don't. I hope you never have to go through what we're going through. I wouldn't say this in front of my wife, but tonight, my life ended when Danielle's did. She was our everything."

Sam placed a hand on his forearm. "Have faith in us to do the right thing for you. Again, we're sorry for your loss."

He stared at her hand and shrugged. "If that's the case, then arrest the person responsible and bloody throw the book at them."

"I promise you, we will. Goodnight, Mr Parker. We'll be in touch soon."

"Make sure you do. I have never appreciated being left in the dark, about *anything*, let alone the slaughter of my beloved family."

Sam decided not to pursue the conversation further and left the house. She marched up the short path and opened the gate.

"Are you all right?" Bob asked, concern written all over his face, lit up in the glow from the streetlights surrounding them.

"Yes, I don't blame him for doubting us, he has a right to want to know the investigation is going to be dealt with professionally and efficiently. I get the impression that if I had dangly bits filling the crotch of my trousers, he would have put his point across differently."

"I was about to say the same thing. I suppose we've got to accept they're both cut up about losing their family. I know I would be traumatised."

"I agree. I think overall, they took the news exceptionally well. And for the record, as I told them, I have no intention of letting either of them down. Right…" Sam glanced at the time on her phone. "Damn, it's twelve-thirty. Okay, let's call it a day and pick up the leads we've gathered in the morning. We've completed all the necessary jobs tonight, now go home and get some rest. I have a feeling we're going to need it in the days ahead of us. See you in the morning, Bob. Drive carefully."

"I'll be fine. Ditto, take care. The number of drink drivers on the road is rising at the moment. No idea where they get their money from. By the time all the bills are paid in my house, the most I can afford for a treat is a KFC around payday."

Sam smiled. "Yeah, right, and what about going out for that Indian meal you mentioned? You do spout a lot of shit at times, but you don't have to be reminded of that, do you?"

"Get out of here and I told you, it was cancelled. I'm off. See you in the morning at nine, if not before."

"I'll be there."

Sam entered her car, and before she drove away from the house, her gaze drifted to the downstairs window at the front. Mrs Parker was in the middle of the room, her head buried in her husband's chest, his arms tightly wrapped around her. She didn't envy them. Sam knew all too well what trauma and heartache would lay ahead of them over the coming days and months until they laid their loved ones to rest.

She drove home on autopilot and snuck into the house. Sonny bounded down the stairs to greet her. After removing her coat and shoes, she got down on her knees and snuggled into his soft fur. "I love you so much, boy. Life can be so cruel at times. I'm glad I have you, Rhys and Casper to come home to. I dread to think what my life would be like if you guys weren't around."

"That's good to know." Rhys surprised her by appearing in the doorway of the lounge.

She hoisted herself to her feet with the aid of the doorframe, her legs full of pins and needles after having a sneaky cuddle with her pooch. She shook them out and then walked towards Rhys. "I thought you'd be tucked up in bed."

"I couldn't sleep, thought I might as well get up and watch the TV."

"Really? That's unusual for you. I caught the news in the car during the drive. That blasted journalist was all over the crime scene again. I had to give her a warning about only dishing out the facts, but it looks like she chose to ignore me. That's another bloody job I'll need to sort out in the morning, putting in a complaint to her boss."

"Will it do any good?" Rhys placed his arms around the back of her neck and pulled her in for a kiss.

She savoured the touch of his lips against hers and then shook her head. "I doubt it but I would be neglecting my duties if I didn't. She's a feisty bitch. I'd like nothing more than to wipe the floor with her but I fear my time will be better spent trying to track down this damned serial killer." She exhaled and then inhaled a larger breath. "That's the second family he's annihilated this week, leaving the husbands alive. Why?"

"The only reasonable explanation I can give is that the perpetrator wants the men to suffer even more than their deceased families."

Sam frowned. "Sorry, I'm not with you. How is that even possible when both their families have been killed?"

He tapped his temple and said, "There's little either of the men can do, with their families gone. I know the first victim was left with horrendous injuries. What about the one this evening?"

"He's got less severe injuries than John Wade, still not good, though. At least he's closer, he's been admitted to Whitehaven Hospital. Bob and I will visit him in the morning, hopefully he'll be conscious by then."

"Another busy day ahead of you tomorrow then."

"Always. I need to get to bed now before I become over-tired and I'm unable to sleep."

"Want me to make you a hot milk or cocoa?"

"No, but it was a lovely thought. Thank you."

They walked up the stairs side by side. Sam discarded her clothes and left them in a pile on the floor. She rarely treated her work clothes that way. Rhys came out of the bathroom and swooped down to collect them. He placed them on the chair in the corner and slipped into the bed beside her.

But as soon as Sam's head hit the pillow, she was gone. Dead to the world.

CHAPTER 7

It was all systems go for Sam at the office the following morning. She arrived early and jotted down a preliminary to-do list that she intended on working her way through during the day.

When the rest of the team showed up for duty, she brought them up to date with the new case.

"I heard about it on the news this morning," Liam said. "The reporter said Cole Thompson was also fighting for his life after being assaulted and maimed by the assailant. Has she got it wrong?" he asked.

"Let's just say she prefers to embellish the truth and leave it there, shall we? Any facts you need to know about the case you ask me and ignore the drivel that woman has to offer, she's talking out of her arse so that she can rise up the promotion ladder swiftly. She told me as much last night when I talked to her about the previous case she had reported on."

"Shameful behaviour," Claire said. "Is there anything that can be done about her? Especially if what she's putting out there lacks any truth, boss?"

"I'm going to do my best to put a stop to it, believe me. That's the first job on my agenda." Sam removed her notebook from her pocket and read out the list she'd made before the team had arrived. "Bob and I will pay the solicitor a visit this morning as well as call in at the hospital to see if Cole has regained consciousness. Claire, I want you to organise a search warrant for the export company's premises. We need to see what's going on there as soon as possible. Oliver, I need you to see what footage you can find from the area. We've got a witness, Ken, who we believe might have caught the perp on a couple of the cameras connected to his doorbell. He's doing his best to obtain the footage and will hopefully be calling in this morning. I had a word with the desk sergeant on the way in, to make him aware of the situation, and asked him to bring the footage straight up when it arrives. I also need the background checks on Cole Thompson and his wife, Danielle. Suzanna, that can be your job for today."

"On it now, boss," Suzanna replied with a nod.

"Alex, do me a favour and check the system, see what you can come up with for both men. Yes, they run a successful export business at present, but there's something niggling me about this, and I think we're missing a vital clue. Let's cover all the possibilities in one go today, ensure we get this investigation off to a good start. I have a feeling Danielle's father is going to make a nuisance of himself until the killer has been caught. I want to be prepared and be able to shoot down any issues he is likely to bombard us with."

"I'll get on it right away."

"We need to check out how many staff the business employs and if there's anything lurking in anyone's past. Liam, why don't you team up with Alex on this one? I think I've given you a lot to cover, and it's imperative we find out this information swiftly. Who's to say he's not still out there, stalking his next victim?"

"God, don't say that. He's hitting them at night, and I could do with some proper sleep tonight. I don't want to get a call-out to attend another murder scene," Bob complained.

Sam jabbed a finger in her partner's direction. "Don't you feel sorry for me, guys? I have to listen to that sort of whingeing all day long."

The team knew better than to respond and put their heads down and got on with their tasks, knowing that Bob sometimes held a grudge if they didn't come down on his side in an argument between them.

"Bloody charming, that is," Bob said. He came closer to Sam who was filling out the whiteboard with the victims' names and relationships. "Could you sleep when you got back into bed this morning?"

"Sorry to disappoint you, but yes, I slept like a baby."

"Great. You're going to be on top form today then, fair play to you. I think you're going to need to give me a nudge at regular intervals throughout the day to ensure I'm still awake."

"Thanks for giving me permission to hit you. I might throw in a sneaky kick here and there, too."

"Nudge I said, not *kick*. Talk about selective hearing. Are we on the move yet? Or are you going to contact the TV station first?"

"The latter, why?"

"I just wanted to know. Okay, in that case, I'll top up our mugs."

"That's the most significant thing I've heard you say all week." Sam winked and swiftly made a beeline for her office before he could retaliate. Ignoring the huge pile of brown envelopes on her desk, she sucked in a few breaths and dug out the number for the local TV station. She'd had to deal with them on a couple of occasions in the past, but that was regarding general enquiries, nothing in this vein. She braced herself for the battle of wills she assumed was about to take place.

Five minutes later, she slammed the phone down and threw a desk tidy at the door.

Seconds later, Bob gingerly stuck his head into the room. "I take it the phone call didn't go well?"

"Not in the slightest. They've got a new boss over there, and guess what?"

"What? Shall I pluck a plausible idea out of the air or are you going to give in and just tell me?"

"All right, give me a break. He brought that bitch with him."

"The reporter? He brought her from where?"

"They were both down south, living and working in the Bath area."

"That explains it, bloody southerners."

Sam laughed. "I'll pretend I didn't hear that."

"Am I wrong?"

She held up a hand to stop him from planting his size tens further in his mouth. "Behave. Anyway, I didn't get very far with him. He told me that she's always proved her worth on his team. Gone above and beyond any other reporters he's worked with, or been in charge of, throughout his career."

"Crikey, that's all well and good, but didn't you tell him what the consequences would be if she chooses to show up at a future crime scene and starts telling porkies?"

"I did. He quoted the Freedom of Speech Act to me verbatim. Tosser."

"I'd be calling him a lot worse, but never in front of a lady."

"Arseholes. You think because you spend ninety percent of the time mumbling, I never catch what you're saying. That couldn't be further from the truth, matey."

"How come your foul moods always come back and bite me in the bum?"

"What? They never do."

He turned sideways and coughed into his hand, and at the same time "Bullshit" tumbled out of his mouth.

"If you've got a problem with me, we need to thrash it out, I've told you this before."

Oliver knocked on the door and poked his head into the room. "Sorry to disturb you, boss."

"You haven't. What's up, Oliver?"

"It's about the bike. We've managed to narrow the list down to three possible owners."

Sam leapt out of her chair. "That's brilliant news. And they all live in Workington?"

"That's right."

"Okay, well, while Bob and I pop out to have a chat with the solicitor, I need you to find out what you can about these three individuals before we pay them a visit."

"Liam's made a start on it already, I just wanted you to be aware."

"Great job."

Oliver backed out of the room, sporting a wide grin.

"Are we friends again now?" she asked her partner.

"I wasn't aware we'd fallen out," Bob said. "Are we going or what?"

Sam rolled her eyes and retrieved her jacket from the back of the chair then followed him out of the office. "We'll be back soon. Keep me updated if you find out anything of interest."

. . .

Sam and Bob entered the solicitor's office. Mr Wilson wore a smart dark-grey pin-striped suit. He welcomed them in the reception area and asked them to accompany him to his office.

"You've caught me between appointments. I usually spend the time typing up notes about the previous client, but that can wait. I get the impression your visit is far more important."

"Thank you, we appreciate you slotting us in at such short notice."

"You're welcome. Carol said that your visit was concerning Danielle Thompson. How can I help?"

"Last night we were called to attend an incident that took place at Danielle's family home."

He stopped twisting the pen through his slender fingers and leaned forward. "Are you telling me that her husband has hurt her? Is that why you're here?"

"We don't believe so. There's no easy way of telling you this, but during the incident, Danielle and her three children were all killed."

"What? No, this can't be true. I know, silly statement after you telling me that, but... this is... utterly shocking. How?"

"We've yet to get a conclusive assessment of the crime scene, but the pathologist's initial assumption is that Cole Thompson was attacked upon his return to the house. We believe he nipped out for a takeaway. In his absence, someone got into the property and slaughtered his family."

"Jesus, I can't believe I'm hearing this. Do you think the husband was involved? Could he have killed his wife and kids and then... wait... how was he attacked?"

"He was beaten and stabbed in the stomach," Sam responded.

"Is it possible he might have caused the injuries himself, *after* killing his family?"

Sam paused to consider the possibility and then shook her head. "On this occasion, I don't think so. We have a witness who possibly saw the killer leaving the scene."

"Damn. How dreadful. Well, I wasn't expecting to hear such grave news at this time of the day. As it happens, I was due to see Danielle this afternoon, to finalise the details of her divorce. You're aware they were separated, I take it?"

"I guessed as much when we searched the house. Danielle's mother confirmed the fact and told us that Danielle was your client, hence our coming to see you today."

"I don't understand, how can I help? Bearing in mind this is all news to me."

"Her mother said the reason for the divorce was irreconcilable differences. I wondered if you wouldn't mind giving us a few more details."

"I don't see why not, especially now my client is deceased. Gosh, I never thought I would be saying those words. She had a zest for life, lived for those children. She told me she fell out of love with Cole a few years ago. Him taking up his role as a partner in the business sealed their fate, if you like."

Sam inclined her head and asked, "May I ask why?"

"I don't suppose there's any point in keeping her files a secret now that she's dead."

"Anything you can tell us will only help us solve the case quicker."

"She came here a few months ago, I remember that day vividly. She was beside herself, broke down when she revealed that she wanted to divorce her husband. She said life had become unbearable, him working all sorts of silly hours, getting called out at two, three and four in the morning. It's not what she signed up for, and she was worried about the impact the strain had put on their marriage and the effect it was having on their children."

"Did she happen to mention what sort of business her

husband dealt with? Sorry, let me ask that in a different way. We're aware that Cole worked for an export company. Did she say what type of exports they managed?"

He glanced out of the window at the stunning, cloudless sky. "She had doubts whether what he was up to was legal. He swore blind it was, but she had her severe reservations that he was telling her the truth. She questioned the type of cargo they were being asked to carry."

Sam chewed on her lip and then said, "That makes sense. Care to enlighten us?"

"Wait a minute... do you believe their deaths had something to do with his business?"

"At this stage of the investigation, we believe it to be a genuine possibility."

"Wow. Can I ask what evidence you have that has led you to that conclusion?"

Sam delayed her response but then chose to reveal the facts about the other on-going case, regarding John Wade and his family. "At the weekend, his partner, John Wade, or should I say his family, also lost their lives in a suspected burglary or break-in."

"Oh heck! And the man himself, this Mr Wade? I take it he survived?"

"He did. Which has highlighted the need for us to delve deeper into the company and what, exactly, they dealt with."

Mr Wilson sat back and raised his hands. "I'll have to stop you there. Danielle didn't divulge any secrets, not in that respect. All she told me was that Cole had been involved in something dodgy and when he confided in her, she felt sick to the stomach, fearing what the consequences would be."

"Unfortunately, we're going to need a lot more than that to go on if we're ever going to learn the truth."

"With respect, Inspector, may I ask why you're not

directing such questions to the husbands, if, as you say, they're both alive?"

"I will be, don't worry. At present, John Wade's life is in the balance, he's been unconscious for a while."

"Sorry to hear that, and Cole Thompson, how's he?"

"He was taken to hospital last night, also unconscious, although his injuries weren't as severe as John's. We chose to let him rest but have every intention of visiting him after we've finished here."

"I see. Well, maybe he'll have the courage of his convictions and tell you what's been going on. I still can't believe that Danielle is no longer with us. What sort of depraved animal can enter someone's home and deliberately take the families' lives like that? It's beyond belief. In all my years of being a solicitor, I don't think I've ever come across anything as bad as this. Maybe it just feels a hundred times worse, dealing with the news, because I knew her, Danielle, and sort of got to know the kids through our brief conversations. She was so proud of them, all of them. Never complained about them. Let's face it, every parent has a minor complaint about their kids at one time or another, but not her. That's why she delayed seeking a divorce for so many years."

"For the sake of the kids. That's so sad. Tell me, was Cole aware that Danielle had come to see you?"

"Yes, he said he would contest nothing and that she and the children could continue to live in the house until the youngest was eighteen, then he agreed it would be sold and the proceeds split fifty-fifty. Danielle felt he was being very fair and that they both wanted the very best for the kids."

"That's why they still both lived at the house, even though they slept in separate bedrooms."

"Yes, she mentioned that had happened a few weeks ago. I believe they were trying to find the right time to tell the children that the marriage was over."

"Makes sense. Do you know much else about the business or Cole's past? We're doing the necessary checks, but I thought I'd see if you could add anything else."

"No, only that they exported a couple of days a week. I believe the ports varied. That's it, I'm afraid."

"Not to worry, I'm sure what you've told us already will help us with the investigation."

"I'm glad, but it won't bring Danielle and her children back, will it?"

Sam swallowed. "No, nothing will do that."

"Have you spoken with anyone else?"

"Only the parents, you know, to break the news. Why?"

"I wondered, that's all."

"I sense there's something else that you're getting at. Please, I need you to be open with me."

"Danielle thought Cole was having an affair with the secretary of the firm."

"Ah, that's an interesting bit of information. I don't suppose you happen to know her name, do you?"

"It's a strange name, one I haven't heard of before. Let me think for a moment or two. Sinta, Sintra, Sinty. It's something along those lines."

"Thanks, we'll get on to it right away." Sam was about to announce they were leaving when her mobile rang. "I'm sorry, I have to get this."

"Of course, there's no need to apologise. It must go off all the time if you're the person in charge of two very difficult investigations."

Sam smiled and answered the call. "DI Sam Cobbs, how can I help?"

"Hello, boss, it's Claire here. Can you speak?"

"Yes, go on, Claire. No, wait, just a minute." Sam decided to take the call outside instead. She mouthed a thank you to Mr Wilson and left his office, presuming that Bob would have the sense to follow her. She walked through the reception area and out into the brilliant sunlight. She leant against the wall and tilted her face up to the sun, keen to benefit from its valuable rays and source of vitamin D. "Okay, I'm outside now, what's up?"

"I wanted you to know right away that the search warrant has been granted for the business premises."

"Super news. Let's get some bodies over there ASAP. I want to drop by the hospital first, see how Cole Thompson is faring, and then Bob and I will shoot over and help with the search. I'm glad you rang. Any luck with finding out about the staff yet?"

"I've got a secretary called Sinty Toolah and four other workers. I could send the names via text, if you like, they're a little hard to get my tongue around."

"Hard to pronounce. Are you telling me they're all foreign?"

"Yes, I don't have to be a genius to tell you that. You'll see when I send them through."

"Great, okay. The reason I mention it is because the witness from last night thought the man we suspect to be the killer spoke with a foreign accent."

"Ah, yes. Okay. There's something else, too. Oliver has also managed to track down the three motorbike owners."

"Yes, he told me that before we left the station. I asked him to do the necessary digging and get back to me. Are you telling me he's found something?"

"Possibly. One of the owners is also foreign. This one I feel confident enough to tackle, it's Jakub Nowak."

"Nowak, does that sound Polish to you?"

"I did a brief search, and yes, it came back as Polish."

"The possibilities are opening up for us then. Either that or they're going to make our lives so much harder. Okay, first things first, we need to get over to the hospital to have a word with Cole Thompson if he's regained consciousness. Do me a favour and check with Carlisle Hospital, see if John Wade's condition has improved at all and get back to me when you can."

"Will get onto them now, boss. Speak later."

Sam popped her phone back into her pocket.

Bob exited the building and smiled. "Sorry, I had to visit the little boys' room. What's going on?"

"Lucky you, I don't have the time."

"You should make time. My mum used to tell me all sorts would happen to my insides if I didn't spend a penny when it was needed."

Sam looked at him and shook her head.

"What have I said now?" he asked.

"Nothing. We need to get on. I sense things are about to get serious."

"Are you going to tell me what you mean by that?"

"I will, yes, in the car. Jump to it, big man, time's a wasting."

CHAPTER 8

The nurse gave them the all-clear to visit Cole, providing they were quiet and refrained from hassling him. Sam eagerly agreed with butterflies in her stomach, her anticipation inching up a notch with every step she took towards the victim's bed on the Men's Ward.

She withdrew her warrant card. "Hello, Mr Thompson. Glad to see you're awake. I'm DI Sam Cobbs, and this is my partner, DS Bob Jones. Are you feeling well enough to speak with us?"

Although he was in a half-sitting position, Sam could tell he was still very sleepy as his eyelids kept drooping.

"Yes and no... why won't anyone tell me why my wife... my wife isn't here with me, sitting beside me?"

Sam hesitated, pondering whether to divulge the truth or not. She decided to see how the conversation went first. "It's not that they don't want to, the nurses probably felt it best not to, for now."

He turned to face her and at the same time his forehead pinched into a frown. He winced in pain and clutched his stomach. "Where is she? I demand to know."

"We have a few questions we'd like to ask you first, sir. About the incident that took place at your home last night." Sam didn't give him a chance to interrupt her, she quickly pressed on, "Am I correct in assuming you went out for a takeaway?"

"That's right. At least I think it is. Everything is a little hazy."

"Can you recollect what happened when you returned to the house?"

"I served up the meals and I think I was taking them through to the lounge... is that where my family were? I can't remember."

"Okay, we'll leave that for now. Was the back door open when you got home? Was there any indication that someone had got into the house in your absence?"

"No, I left the back door unlocked while I was out, I always do that. I was shocked when this person jumped out on me."

"They were hiding?"

"Yes, the little door under the stairs was open, maybe he tucked himself away in there and waited for the right moment to attack me."

"Okay, we can pass that information on to the forensic team who are still going over the crime scene."

"How long have I been out? Unconscious, I mean?"

"Since the attack occurred last night. Do you know what injuries you sustained?"

"Yes, they said the fucker stabbed me. I'm covered in bruises around my torso. They also believe this person gave me a good kicking. A scan revealed that my kidneys are bruised."

"Did you see the intruder? Could you identify them?"

"No, he, I'm presuming it was a bloke, he was wearing a balaclava. It all happened out of the blue, the element of surprise. He took the wind out of my sails, floored me before I had the chance to fight back, and then nothing… everything went blank, and I passed out. Please, I need to know about my family, just tell me they're all right."

Witnessing the confusion in his eyes and sensing he was strong enough to accept the news, she inhaled a deep breath and placed a hand over his. "I'm sorry, your family didn't make it."

He stared at her for what seemed like an age and then passed out.

"Shit! I wasn't expecting that. Christ, I hope his heart hasn't conked out."

"Fuck, I'll get the nurse." Bob tore at the curtain.

His footsteps drifted off into the distance and then got louder again upon his return. The nurse threw back the curtain and demanded they leave. Another nurse arrived, and they drew the curtains together again, shielding Sam's view of Cole. Deflated, she made her way back to the nurses' station and waited for the nurses to deal with the patient. It took a while, but eventually the two women returned to their station.

"Well? How is he?"

"Before we tell you that, I need to know what you told him that caused him to pass out," the older of the two nurses asked.

Sam held her head in shame. "Sorry, he kept asking why his wife wasn't there with him. In the end, I felt obliged to tell him the truth."

The older nurse tutted, rounded the desk and sat. "I can't believe you did that. We were biding our time, ensuring he was strong enough after his surgery before we told him the news."

"I'm sorry. I regret my actions, but he kept on and on

about his wife and he sounded strong enough, so I took the chance and told him. Is he all right?"

"It wasn't your decision to make, he's in *our* care and we're here to ensure he is fit enough to cope with such devastating news. It's all right for the likes of you to walk in off the street and speak with him for five minutes and then go off on your merry way. We're the ones who have to deal with the consequences. Why can't you people understand and respect the advice we give you?"

"I'm truly sorry. I'll know better next time. It's just that we have a serial killer on the loose who we're desperate to capture before they kill anyone else. Surely you can see this from my point of view."

"That's all well and good, but I specifically told you not to hassle him, didn't I?"

"Yes, you did. I can't keep apologising. How is he?" Sam asked for what must have been the third time.

"He's back with us, no thanks to you."

"Can I see him, you know, to apologise?"

"Absolutely not. You'd be wise to leave now. If you don't, I'll be forced to call security after what you've put him through."

Sam had never been spoken to like that before, not by a member of staff at any hospital she'd had the misfortune to visit during an investigation over the years, and it hurt. In fact, she felt ashamed and utterly humiliated. She did the only thing left open to her, turned her back on the nurse who had taken pleasure in reprimanding her and exited the ward. There was an officer on duty in the hallway.

"Keep an eye on him. Any issues, ring my personal number, got that?" She handed him one of her business cards and trotted down the narrow corridor to the lift at the end.

"Hey, wait for me." Bob trotted to catch up with her.

Sam jabbed at the button several times to summon the lift.

"What the fuck...? You're going to need to calm down."

Sam's mobile rang. Her heart raced, and her pulse beat out a rhythm to match any drums on a battlefield. The lift opened, and she entered, then answered the call. "DI Sam Cobbs."

"Inspector, it's Claire. Just calling to give you an update on John Wade."

"I hope it's good news, I could sure do with some right now."

"It's not, sorry. They've decided his body needs more time to recover from the injuries he's suffered, so they're intending to keep him in an induced coma for the next day or two."

"Damn. He must be worse than they first thought. Okay, thanks, Claire. Who has gone over to start the search at the business premises?"

"Liam and Oliver volunteered. Leaving the three of us to continue slotting all the pieces together at this end. I do have some good news for you."

"I'm eager to hear what that is. Things haven't gone too well with Cole Thompson."

"Sorry to hear that, boss. Alex thinks he's managed to track down a rogue consignment of gas canisters that came into the country via Poland."

"Okay, that really is putting all the pieces together, isn't it? Anything else showing up on this Nowak?"

"I've got an address for him, if you want it?"

"Yes, give it to me. Bob and I will try and find him before we join the others at the export company. Can you also fire over the address for that as well?"

"I'll pop both addresses on a text now. Chin up, boss, I can sense how down you are."

"I'm all right. Don't worry about me. It does me good to get a dressing down now and again, it keeps me grounded."

"Eek... I believe you. Firing the information over pronto."

Sam ended the call, and almost instantly her mobile pinged. She opened the message and took note of both addresses then angled her phone at Bob. "Nowak's address. We'll head over there before going to meet up with the others."

"Suits me. Are you all right?"

"I will be. I needed to get out of there. I don't hold it against the nurse for putting me in my place, but bloody hell, that stung."

"I felt for you. You held off long enough. The poor guy was getting more and more worked up about his wife, it was only a matter of time before the news came out."

"It's over and done with now. I'm just pissed off I didn't get more out of him about the business. We'll still need to revisit him in the near future, something that I will be reluctant to do, thanks to Miss Bossy Knickers back there."

Bob chuckled and then apologised. "Sorry, I shouldn't laugh, but your face was a picture."

"Glad my mortification has been the highlight of your day so far, partner," she uttered stiffly.

THEY ARRIVED at the first address. It was a large detached building, that, according to the bell system at the main front door, had been turned into eight flats. Sam pressed Nowak's number, but there was no response.

"Did you really think he would open the door for you?"

"If he's got nothing to hide, yes." Sam peered over her shoulder at the designated parking area. "I can't see a bike there. Presumably, he's out."

"Might be worth checking around the back or at the side, in case he parks it there instead."

"Good call."

There was a small opening at the side of the building. Sam led the way, and that's where they found the bike, towards the back of the house, covered in a silver rainproof sheet.

"Bingo," Bob shouted.

"So, he's either got the use of another vehicle or he's inside, aware that we're out here."

"I'm inclined to think the latter. What do you want to do?"

Sam paused to consider the options, keen to get to their next port of call. "We need to set up a surveillance on the flat, just in case."

"Who are you going to get to do it?"

"Let's get over to the business premises and see how many bodies are there first, then I'll make the call."

"And in the meantime?"

Sam removed her phone from her pocket and rang the station. "Hi, Claire, it's me. We're at Nowak's address, and the bike is here, it's covered. He's either refusing to open the door to us or he's out. Can you check, see if there are any other vehicles registered to him at this address?"

"Will do, boss. I was about to give you a call. The chap with the USB of the footage you were expecting has just dropped it off. He apologised for the delay but said he had problems locating the manual and he's hopeless with technology."

"Not to worry. Can anyone spare the time to go through it for me, or is that asking too much with the tasks I've already set you guys?"

"I'm sure we can manage, boss. Leave it with me."

"Okay, we're going to hop in the car and join the others now."

"I'll be in touch if there's anything else to report."

Sam returned her phone to her pocket and retraced her steps to the front of the building to find a woman, carrying shopping, about to enter the main entrance. Sam produced her ID. "Hi, sorry to interrupt. Can you tell me if you know Jakub Nowak? He lives at number four."

Puzzled, the woman placed her carrier bags on the ground and glanced up at the window above. "His flat is the one at the front. That one there. I can't say I've seen him for a few days, but that's not uncommon. I work shifts at a nursing home, so I'm not really around much. He parks that damned bike of his at the side if that's any help?"

"Yes, we noticed. Does he have access to another vehicle?"

Her mouth twisted as she thought. "I can't be a hundred percent sure, I'm sorry."

"Not to worry. I don't suppose you'd be willing to let us in so we can see if he's up there, would you?"

"Of course. Has he done something wrong?"

"No, we're just making enquiries to do with an investigation we're working on."

"I see. Come with me."

"Bob, help the lady with her bags, will you?"

Her partner swooped down and effortlessly picked up the four bags. The woman gave him a thankful toothy smile.

"Handy having a hunk like him around, I should imagine."

Sam's eyes widened, and she resisted the temptation to let out a laugh. "Makes my day, it's so handy, having him at my beck and call," she replied.

She winked at Bob who she could tell was seething.

The woman let them into the property and then led the way up the wide mahogany staircase. The entrance hall was a grand open space, a shard of daylight filling it from a large window on the landing above.

"Has this place been renovated long?" Sam asked.

"A couple of years. The landlord vets the tenants well, so we don't get any riffraff living here. Saying that, Nowak's bike causes a certain amount of irritation amongst the tenants at times."

"They can be a nightmare to deal with, I agree."

At the top of the stairs, the woman relieved Bob of the carrier bags. "This is mine here, and Nowak's is just around the corner, on the right."

"We appreciate your help, thanks again."

"No, thank you for carrying the heavy bags upstairs for me. I'm usually all puffed out by the time I get up here," the woman said.

She flashed another bright smile at Bob who shuffled his feet, embarrassment setting in.

The woman let herself into her flat, and Sam dug him in the ribs.

"You little hero, you."

"Bollocks. All in the line of duty."

Sam dipped around the corner and knocked on Nowak's door. It remained unanswered. Deflated, they left the area and returned to the car.

"What a waste of time that was," Bob grumbled.

"Even with all that hero-worshipping to brighten your day?"

"Whatever," he replied grumpily behind her as they made their way back down the stairs.

NEXT STOP WAS the office of the export business. When they got there, Sam was delighted, yet puzzled, to see the door intact and not smashed down by her colleagues. It wasn't until she entered the office that she realised why. Sitting at a desk in the corner of the room was a blonde. Her long, bare legs looked tanned as if she'd recently travelled abroad.

Oliver saw them arrive and crossed the room towards them. "This is the secretary, Sinty. She insisted she should stay here. I couldn't think of a reason why she shouldn't be here, boss. I hope I've done the right thing, not kicking her out?"

"It's fine. As long as she doesn't get in the way and hamper our progress."

Oliver leaned in and whispered, "Let's just say she's keeping a watchful eye on us while pretending she's not."

"I'm with you. We've got a dilemma on our hands."

"What's that, boss?" Oliver asked.

"We've been to Nowak's flat and found the motorbike under cover near the rear of the property. A neighbour let us in through the main entrance, and we knocked on the door to his flat but didn't receive an answer."

"And you think it would be a good idea if a couple of us set up a surveillance over there to await his return?"

Sam placed a finger on the tip of her nose. "You've got it. Claire's checking if Nowak has any other vehicles registered at that address. Until we get that information, we're stumped."

"I don't mind venturing over there. We have more than enough bodies here."

There were four uniformed officers assisting Liam to carry on the search.

"Makes sense. Why don't you take Liam with you? Bob and I can oversee things here, and I can interview the secretary at the same time."

"As you wish. Liam, we're off."

Liam came to join them. "Is something wrong?"

"I'll fill you in on the way," Oliver said.

"Give me a call as soon as anything crops up over there," Sam said.

Liam and Oliver left the office.

"You continue the search with the others, and I'll try and keep the secretary distracted."

"What if she's hiding something in her desk? Maybe that's why she's refusing to leave. Or," Bob leaned in closer, "maybe her desk is positioned over a trap door or loose floorboards and that's why she's staying put."

"The possibilities are endless, aren't they? You leave her to me."

Sam smiled and made her way across the room to where the secretary was typing at the computer. "Sorry about all of this, I'm DI Sam Cobbs. You're Sinty, aren't you? Did I pronounce that right?"

"Yes, you did. What's all this about? All the officers would tell me was they had a right to be here and showed me the search warrant. But I don't understand what you could be looking for."

"Have you worked here long, Sinty?"

"Yes, two years. John Wade took me on when I was desperate to find work."

"Desperate? What work were you doing at the time?"

"I was a barmaid at his local pub. We got talking, and he asked me if I could do any job in the world, what would it be. I told him I wanted to run my own business one day. And he offered me an opportunity to learn the ropes around here."

"So you're more than just a secretary then?"

"Indeed. But I'm still the one who carries out most of the office work."

"How well do you get on with John and Cole?"

Sinty's cheeks coloured up at the mention of Cole's name.

"They're both very friendly, good men, they are."

"In what way?" Sam pressed.

"I don't understand."

"Rumour has it that you and Cole are an item, is that correct?"

"I... umm... who told you that?"

"I've forgotten. Is it true?"

"Yes, it's true. We're going to be together soon, once he leaves his wife."

"How long have you been seeing one another?"

"Around four months. We just clicked when he began working here."

"And you started an affair, despite knowing that he was married?"

Sinty's head lowered slightly. "It wasn't something either of us planned. It's hard to prevent feelings from developing and taking over your existence. I tried not to get involved, but he's a lovely man. Hey, his marriage was on the rocks before I came along, he'll tell you that."

"I'm sure. I've yet to interview him about your affair. Do you know what's been going on this week?"

She frowned and picked up a pen to keep her hands busy, twisting it between her fingers. "Not really. John hasn't been in for a few days. Cole and I have tried to contact him, but he isn't returning our calls. Cole was due in at nine this morning, and now he's nowhere to be seen. Again, I've left a number of messages on his phone, but he hasn't got back to me. I was shocked when your men showed up. Please, won't you tell me what's going on? I'm scared and also worried sick about John and Cole."

It was a tough call for Sam to make. Did she reveal all at this early stage or did she start getting heavy with the woman from the get-go, in the hope that she might crumble and disclose what type of setup was going on there? "Okay, this is against my better judgement, but I'm hopeful that if I tell you the truth, you'll fill in a few blanks we have."

"I don't understand. The truth? Has something happened to John and Cole?"

Sam nodded. "Unfortunately, both men are in hospital at the moment."

She dropped the pen, and her hands flattened against both of her cheeks. "My God, how can that be? Were they involved in accidents?"

Sam wondered if Sinty was a convincing actress or whether she was genuinely oblivious to what was going on. "You could say that. Sometime over the weekend, John's home was broken into, his family were all killed, and he was left for dead. He's in hospital. The staff are doing their best to save his life."

"Shit! That's terrible news. I've got a feeling I'm going to regret asking this: what happened to Cole?"

"Much the same. We believe while he was out, picking up a takeaway, someone got into his home, killed his family, and then attacked him upon his return."

"No… this can't be true. His family is gone?"

"That's right, all dead. All butchered at the hands of a vile individual."

"Who? Do you know? Wait, what about Cole? How is he?"

"We visited him at the hospital this morning. He's recovering, although he was devastated to hear the news about his family," Sam fibbed, keen to see what her reaction would be.

"That's obvious. Oh shit, that poor man, but he's going to be all right? He wasn't badly injured, was he?"

"He was stabbed in the stomach and needed an operation to repair the damage. I think he's going to be in there a while. Hence us turning up here today."

"I don't understand. I'm sorry, my mind is all over the place. If I'm missing something obvious here, you're going to have to be more open with me."

"We believe the attacks have something to do with the

business. Now, given what I've already told you, is there anything important you believe we should know about?"

"Know about? In what sense?" Her gaze shifted to the desk.

Sam expelled a frustrated breath. "I thought we were getting somewhere, apparently not."

"I'm not being obstructive on purpose, I just don't know what to tell you. I want to help, but you're going to have to be clear about what you're asking me."

"Okay, let's get down to the nitty-gritty here. What sort of exports does the company deal with?"

"Anything and everything."

"We have reason to believe that some of it might be a bit dodgy, is that true?"

Again, Sinty's gaze shifted, this time to a spot at the back of the room.

It was then that Bob shouted for Sam to join him. She crossed the room to the filing cabinet in the corner to see what her partner had discovered. "Burners?"

Bob held two mobile phones in his gloved hands.

"Probably. Want me to get them over to the lab?"

"Can you try and open them first?"

"I've tried, they're locked."

"That figures. Let me see what she has to say about them."

Bob put the phones in two separate Ziplock bags and handed them to Sam, who then returned to Sinty.

"Care to tell me about these, Sinty?"

"Umm... what do you want to know?"

"For a start, who do they belong to."

"I don't know. I've never seen them before. I didn't even know they existed."

Exasperation set in. Sam stared at her for a long time, hoping to unsettle the woman, make her crumble and tell her the truth. "Really? You never knew they were there?"

"No, why should I know?"

"They were found at the bottom of a filing cabinet. Next you'll be telling me you never use that cabinet."

"I don't, not really. Not with the new software we've had installed lately. There's no need to keep paper copies of any files now."

Sam smiled. "In that case, we're going to have to seize your computer."

"But you can't, I need it for work."

"With the partners both in hospital, I'm assuming your contracts will dry up over the coming weeks."

"No, that's not how it works. We have consignments coming in all the time, sometimes they are booked four to six months ahead. We're busy most weeks."

"I'm sure you'll cope somehow. We'll give you a chance to print out the docking manifests or whatever you need to oversee the exports. I'll assist you to do that."

"I don't need any help to do my job, especially from the police."

"Then you'd better get on with it." Sam pulled up a chair alongside her and watched Sinty deal with the export schedule for the next few months. Sam refused to take her eyes off the screen, unnerving the woman in the process.

Sinty made several mistakes and cursed under her breath.

"I caught an accent then. Where are you from, Sinty?"

"Poland, but I haven't lived there in decades. I arrived here as a child, when I was four. My parents thought it would be better to allow me to learn English properly and not to speak Polish at home, but my sister and brother agreed that we should practice on our own in case we were ever deported."

"Why would you be deported? Are you here illegally?"

"No, not us. Not my family. But you never know if the government will change its policies."

Sam's suspicions grew. "But you know others who have come here illegally, am I right?"

Sinty remained silent for a while.

"Sinty? If you don't tell me the truth, and I find out you've been lying to me, I can arrest you. Surely that will bring shame on your family, won't it?"

"Yes, no, I won't allow you to do that. Yes, I know others."

A lightbulb went off in Sam's head. "And how do these illegal people come into the country?"

Bob came and stood beside Sam. He was holding some kind of ledger. "I found this taped to the bottom of one of the drawers."

"Please, I know nothing. Don't blame this on me. I had nothing to do with it," Sinty pleaded, tears bulging and sliding down her colourless cheeks.

"Come now, you don't expect us to believe you, do you?" Sam replied. She snapped on a pair of gloves and flicked through the ledger. "Dates and expected cargo. That'll do for me, Bob. I think this has sealed the company's fate and those of the employees, unless Sinty does the right thing and decides to work with us instead of against us. How about it, Sinty? Will you be willing to do that?"

She fell forward, rested her forehead on her arm and sobbed. Sam glanced up to see the uniformed officers turn their way, knowing smirks on their faces.

Sam showed the woman minimal sympathy and patted her on the back gently. "Come now, less of the tears. You have nothing to fear if you're prepared to tell us the truth."

Sinty sat upright and wiped her nose on the cuff of her cardigan, something that had always repulsed Sam.

"I will cooperate. My parents will disown me if they learn the truth."

"Which is? The company has been trafficking people, hasn't it?"

The young woman sniffled and nodded. "Yes, that's right. Not often, but when times are slack, John gets in touch with one of his contacts, and he calls it 'easy money'."

"Easy money, ferrying people into this country for what purpose? To work in the slave trade?"

Her head dipped once more. "Yes, sometimes. Polish people are good workers, but they can't find jobs in Poland."

"So you guys dangle the carrot, entice them to travel with you, no doubt for an extortionate fee."

She shook her head. "No fee."

"What? Oh, I get it, they come here destitute, work all the hours under the sun and hand over their money to you, to pay off the fees incurred for the trip to England. How did I do?"

"Yes, you're right, except for one thing."

"Surprise me," Sam said sarcastically.

"I wasn't involved. Not initially. It wasn't until Cole and I started dating that I learnt about any of this."

Sam cocked an eyebrow. "Don't try and pull the wool over my eyes, Sinty. You're up to your neck in this. I've been observing you since we arrived, you've been on tenterhooks, looking shifty."

"Tenderhooks, yes," she said, mispronouncing the word. "Wouldn't you be, if the police turned up to raid your place of work?"

"I'll give you that one. Right, now we need to get down to what's really going on here. Why do you think both John and Cole, and their families, have been targeted? Has something drastic happened in the past couple of weeks?"

Sinty covered her eyes with her shaking hand. "Yes, but I can't tell you."

"Okay, I've heard enough. Cuff her, Bob, we'll continue this interview back at the station."

"No, no, I don't want to go, please don't make me go to that place."

"What's to fear about going to the police station?"

"In my country, people rarely come out of such places unharmed. Once the police have you behind closed doors, they rape the women and beat the men."

"Not in this country. That's why you and your fellow countrymen are so keen to move here, isn't it? To be treated fairly?"

"Without a doubt, we just want to be considered like human beings."

"And you will be, if you tell me the truth. If you're not prepared to do that here then we need to take you in for questioning, it's your call."

"But why?"

"Why what? I've already explained why you need to come to the station. Sitting here questioning my authority is doing you no good. Now, are you going to tell me what happened a few weeks ago?"

Sinty fidgeted uncomfortably, her gaze darting around the room to each of the officers involved in the search. "I can't. There are other people involved, dangerous people. They'll come here and hurt me, I know they will."

"Do you believe these people are the ones who have gone after John and Cole? Who have killed their families?"

Sinty ran a hand around her face and tugged at her ear before she answered. "Possibly."

"Possibly? You have a reason to believe it might be someone else?" Sam took a punt and followed up with another question she was eager to know the answer to. "Do you know the name Jakub Nowak?"

The way the young woman's eyes widened and she swallowed was all the confirmation Sam needed.

"How do you know him?" Sam asked.

"Why? Why do I have to answer all of these questions? I know nothing, I told you that from the beginning."

Sam rose from her seat and said, "Bob, I've heard enough. Cuff her, we'll deal with this in the interrogation room back at the station."

Fear suddenly materialised in her watery eyes, and Sinty's hands shook violently. "Interrogation room? You mean you're going to torture me until I tell you the truth."

"Sorry, my mistake, call it a slip of the tongue, I meant interview room. It's entirely up to you. All of that can be avoided if you speak openly with us, here and now."

"Oh God! John and Cole are going to kill me. I wish you would speak to them first. I don't want to step on anyone's toes, say the wrong thing."

Sam's irritation soared. "May I remind you that the two men are in hospital and their families have been slaughtered, surely that outweighs everything else. For example, your reluctance to be honest with me."

She sat in silence for several seconds then shook her head and said, "May God forgive me."

"For what?"

"For all of this, getting involved with Cole in the first place. If I hadn't, I'd be none the wiser." She paused and gasped. "What if I'm next? What if someone comes here to take me out? No, you can't allow this to happen, you just can't."

"You see, there lies my dilemma. If you refuse to open up to us, then I'm quite within my rights to either arrest you or to walk away. But, on the other hand, if you choose to be honest with me, then there are measures I can put in place to protect you."

"You'd do that for me?"

"Yes, providing you're fair with me."

"Then I have no option but to trust you. I feel my life is in grave danger, if only by association."

"If we're going to sort you out with protection then it would be better if we interviewed you at the station. You'll be safe there, I promise."

After another pause, Sinty opened the drawer to the side of her and withdrew her handbag. "Okay, I'm ready to go. Shall I leave the key of this place with the officers?"

"Yes, they'll ensure it's locked up securely. Before we leave, is there anything else we should know? What about a safe perhaps?"

"Yes, there is one. But only John and Cole have access to it."

"Are you aware of how much money they keep in it?"

"A fair amount, I think. Although they never discuss such matters with me."

Sinty surprised Sam by breaking down. Racking sobs filled the room, and again the other officers peered over their shoulders. Sam gestured for them to get back to work.

She placed a hand over Sinty's. "It's okay, we'll get you through this, if you trust us."

"I said I will. But it's still daunting."

"What is?" Sam asked.

"Knowing what these people are capable of. I have my family to consider, my mother, father and sister. I should warn them, tell them to remain vigilant and ask them to look out for each other."

"That might not be such a bad idea. Yes, do that now."

Sam stepped away from the young woman, allowing her the privacy needed to make the call.

Bob got close, one eye on Sinty behind her, and said, "You're being too trusting. How do we know she's not involved in the murders? She was shagging one of them. It's easy to blame someone else and bump the wife and kids off at the same time."

Sam glanced back at the terrified woman. "I don't think so. Instinct is telling me she knows more than she's letting on, though, hence our need to get her out of here and back to the station. However, I need to work on her some more first. Maybe there's other evidence hidden around here that she might highlight before we leave. We need to gather all we can to make this one stick in court. That's my belief anyway."

"Yep, on that we agree. If we can get her away from the desk, I still reckon there might be something under there that she's doing her best to hide from us. I don't trust her, not as much as you do."

"When we transfer her to the car, I'll get her settled while you and the others do the necessary searching, in and around the desk, then join us in the car."

"Sounds good to me."

Sam returned to find Sinty clutching something in her hand. "What's that?"

"My rosary beads. I'm searching for God's forgiveness and support, to keep my family safe from harm."

"I understand. What about your family? Did you manage to contact them?"

"Yes, they're together. I told them I will be in touch later, if I can. They're scared, so am I."

"There's no reason for you to be scared, you're safe while you're with us, I promise."

"I hope so."

Sam led the way out to the car and placed Sinty in the back. "We won't be long. My partner is running through a few details with the men inside, and then we'll be off."

"Okay, that's fine by me." Sinty searched the area around her, glancing over her shoulder now and again.

Sam tried to use the woman's fear to her advantage. "Why don't you tell me how you know Jakub Nowak?"

After more peering over her shoulder, Sinty finally said, "He came to the office last week, he was distraught."

"Why?" Sinty sighed.

Sam could sense her hesitation. "Come now, you need to be honest with me if we're going to get anywhere."

Sinty's head tipped back, and she let out a guttural moan. "Because his family perished on a trip to the UK."

"*What?* Are you telling me his family were being trafficked and they died while in your care?"

"Not mine, no, this has nothing to do with me, I keep telling you that."

"All right, let me rephrase that, at the hands of the company?"

"Yes. They were travelling by boat, and it capsized, off the coast of the Isle of Wight."

Sam thought back to any news bulletins she had caught regarding immigrants dying on the coastline in the past few weeks or months.

"They were coming from Poland or making their way from somewhere else?"

"From France. The French don't care, they let the boats set off, knowing that when they land, they would become the UK's problem instead of theirs."

Sam thought as much. She had heard stories about the French police even towing some boats out to sea to get them off to a clear start, off the rugged coastline.

Bob opened the passenger door and startled Sam.

"Jesus, you scared me witless. Anything?"

"Nope, I was mistaken." He clicked his seat belt in place.

Sam did the same and turned the key in the ignition. "Right, let's get back to the station."

. . .

When they arrived, Sam asked the desk sergeant to make Sinty as comfortable as possible in an interview room and ensure she had a drink to hand. Sam ran up the stairs to the incident room to inform the team about what they'd discovered at the export firm.

"While Bob and I are interviewing Sinty, Claire, I'd like you to go through the ledger we found, see if you can make any sense of it. Any news from the boys yet?"

Claire took the ledger from Sam. "Nothing as yet. Looks like things are coming together."

"It does. I'm cautious, but I refuse to get too excited. I'll do that once Jakub Nowak is in custody. Then, and only then, will I be able to let out a relieved sigh. If his family died on a boat, then he must be a very confused person, and no, that's not me making excuses for him. It's a fact. He must have been driven to killing the Wades and the Thompsons out of sheer desperation. Maybe tinged with a touch of revenge thrown into the mix, too."

"It's horrendous. So many needless lives are lost this way. We're an island, we can't man every damn inch of the coastline, and these unscrupulous people are aware of it and capitalising on the fact," Claire stated.

"I agree, but it's all about greed at the end of the day. The victims' houses are proof of that, if ever it were needed."

"Shame on them, but look where it has got them in the end," Bob chipped in.

"Exactly. Greed does not conquer all. There are too many obstacles in the way to overcome before the money ends up in the safe or in their back pockets, anything to avoid paying tax. Right, I'm going to see what else I can get out of her now that she's had a chance to rethink her clearly untenable position." Sam poured herself and Bob a coffee and handed him a mug. "We'll take these with us."

"Good luck," Claire called out.

They found Sinty Toolah staring into the mug grasped in her slender hands, her head bowed.

"Gosh, I didn't think you would bring me back here and just dump me."

"It's only been ten minutes, Sinty. I needed to bring my team up to date on the investigation."

"I feel too enclosed in here, claustrophobic even. Can we not do this elsewhere?"

"I'm sorry. I would offer to conduct this interview in my office, except the general public aren't allowed past the security door, for obvious reasons."

"It's okay. Can we get on with it? I'm desperate to get back to my family."

"Of course."

Sam and Bob settled into their seats opposite her, and the interview began with Bob saying the usual verbiage to get the recording underway. Sam was aware of the need to repeat herself to get the information recorded.

"If we can go over a few minor details about what goes on at the company you work for, Worldwide Exports? Can you tell us what your involvement in the business is?" Sam asked.

"I'm an associate, much more than just a secretary, although I'm the one who carries out the menial tasks such as arranging the shipments, typing up the relevant reports and ensuring everything runs smoothly."

"How many exports does the company have every month?"

"Up to about fifty."

"And are all those transactions legal?"

Sinty squeezed her eyes closed and shook her head.

"Sorry, Miss Toolah, for the purpose of the recording, you're going to need to speak the words not just shake your head."

"No, now and again we have to find other ways of bringing in the cash."

"And that involves trafficking people, is that correct?"

Sinty nodded.

"You're nodding, please can you answer the question? I'll repeat it for you: that involves trafficking people, is that correct?"

"Yes, sometimes."

"How do these crossings take place?"

"Sometimes via road, via ships in containers, and sometimes via small boats."

"Boats so small that they are often overloaded and capsize, right?"

"Yes, that sometimes happens, regretfully."

"And an incident like that occurred a few weeks ago, off the coast of the Isle of Wight, didn't it?"

Sinty fell silent for a second or two until Sam prompted her for a response.

"Didn't it?"

"Yes, tragedy struck, and sadly a lot of lives were lost."

"How many?"

"Around fifty, I believe."

"And all of those people paid the company good money upfront to get into the country under the radar, so to speak?"

"No."

"No? How did it work then?"

"The company paid the people to transport the immigrants, and they would then be taken to a place to live and work until their fares were paid off."

"How much are we talking about here? A couple of hundred pounds?"

Sinty sighed. "Hardly, more like five thousand for each person."

Sam sat back and sighed. "So these people who were

destitute came to you, begging to save them, and your company took advantage of them?"

"Not *my* company," Sinty reminded her. "I only work there. John Wade and Cole Thompson are the ones who benefit from the profits, not me."

"Ah, but aren't you and Cole Thompson an item now? He separated from his wife a little while ago because he and you started an affair, didn't you?"

"Yes, that's right. We started seeing each other a few months ago. His marriage was over by then. I'm not a marriage-wrecker, I swear I'm not."

"How do you know Jakub Nowak?"

"He came to the office last week. He was very upset and caused a scene."

"Why?"

"Because all of his family were on the boat that capsized off the coast of the Isle of Wight."

"That must have been heartbreaking for him. Why didn't he report it to the police?"

"Because they were coming to the UK illegally."

"Are you aware that John Wade and Cole Thompson are both in hospital?"

"I am now, you told me as much at the office before you brought me here. Until then, I had no knowledge of this at all. Or about what happened to their families."

"Yes, the rest of their families were all slaughtered by someone who broke into their homes. Did you have anything to do with the attacks?"

The question shocked Sinty. She vigorously shook her head. "No, no, I had nothing to do with this. How can you sit there and suggest such a thing?"

"Don't you think it's strange that Cole separates from his wife, their divorce is imminent, and it has been agreed that Cole should move out of the family home and yet, within a couple of days of that agreement coming to the table, Cole's wife and three children are all brutally murdered in their own home?"

"No, I won't allow you to pin this on me. I had nothing to do with it. Oh God, I feel sick that you should even think such a thing. I'm not as heartless as that."

"Maybe not, but you worked for a firm that primarily brought people illegally into this country."

"Not primarily, that's not what I told you. Anyway, I only recently found out about that side of things. John and Cole were very secretive regarding the arrangements they put in place."

"And when you started seeing Cole, he revealed the true facts about the business and how it all worked?"

"Yes. The trafficking only took place *occasionally*, when business was slow."

"When did it begin? Do you know?"

"I think not long after the pandemic. John got involved with some nasty villains, and they coerced him into the dodgy dealings. He was overwhelmed by requests and brought Cole into the company."

"And yet you told me that you knew nothing about the trafficking, not until you started dating Cole. You really expect me to believe that?"

"Yes, because it's the truth," Sinty cried in anguish.

"The people who capsized in the boat off the Isle of Wight, what nationality were they?"

"A mixture of Polish, Belgians and Croatians, I think."

"And where do you hail from, Sinty?"

"Poland. My family came here decades ago."

"Don't you think it's strange that you being a Polish national…?"

Sinty stopped her by wagging her finger and glaring at Sam. "No, you can't blame me for this, any of it. Just because some of the people were from Poland, it doesn't mean that I had anything to do with it."

"How many of Nowak's relatives died that day?"

"Six, his wife and five children."

Sam's heart sank. "What did he say when he came to the office?"

"He started swearing and shouting at Cole and John. They sent me out to get some rolls for lunch, so I'm not really sure what else was said. When I returned from running my errand, the man had gone."

"How convenient."

Sinty slammed her clenched fist on the table. "It's the truth, I tell you, the truth. What reason would I have to lie now that this is all out in the open?"

Sam didn't get the chance to reply because there was a knock on the door. She left her seat to answer it and slipped out of the room when she saw Suzanna standing in the hallway.

"Sorry to interrupt, boss, Claire thought you should be told right away."

"Told what?"

"We've just received a call from Jessica Connor."

"John Wade's sister? No, don't tell me he's dead."

"No, it's nothing to do with John Wade. She asked to speak with you urgently. I said you couldn't be disturbed as you were interviewing a possible suspect. It was then that she broke down in tears."

Sam gestured for Suzanna to get to the point.

"I'm sorry, I wanted you to be aware of all the facts first. She told me her daughter had been kidnapped."

CHAPTER 9

Sam slammed against the wall, the unexpected news knocking the wind out of her. "Shit, could she give you any further details?"

"No, she said her daughter went missing during her lunchbreak at school. She nipped out to the chippy. Her friends returned, but she didn't. When the teacher asked where Marnie had got to, her friends said that a man showed up and told Marnie to get in the car as her mother had been injured and was asking for her at the hospital."

"Fuck. Did the kids say if the man had an accent?"

"If he did, the message wasn't passed back to Jessica. She's going frantic. I said you'd give her a call as soon as you could."

"Thanks. All right, we're nearly done with Toolah. I'll get her booked in, more for her own safety, although I think CPS will want to throw accessory charges at her once her story comes out. I'll be up shortly and I'll give Jessica a call back. Have you checked in with Liam and Oliver lately?"

"I can do that when I get back to my desk, boss."

"Okay, if they haven't seen him then tell them to return to

base. No, forget that, they should remain outside the flat in case he takes the girl back there, if Nowak is guilty of abducting Marnie. Give them a ring, make them aware of the situation."

"Okay, boss."

Sam watched Suzanna trot up the corridor, her mind whirling like a tornado had taken up residence inside her head. *Jesus, I was not expecting this. What if we can't find the girl in time? Bearing in mind what the killer has already done to Wade's family, and Thompson's for that matter. I don't hold out much hope of finding Marnie alive. Of course, I have no intention of telling her mother that. What a frigging mess! Shit, shit, shit!*

She re-entered the interview room. Bob's gaze met hers. She could tell that he instantly knew something was wrong, despite Sam doing her utmost to disguise her emotions.

She sat in her seat, looked Sinty in the eye and announced, "Please forgive me, but something urgent has come up that needs my attention. I'm going to have to leave this interview here for now."

"What? You can't do this to me. Treat me like a nobody."

"I'm hardly doing that. As I've already said, I'm needed elsewhere. It could be a matter of life and death, and we've already had far too many deaths for my liking this week. You'll be put in a cell, for your own safety, until more suitable arrangements can be made for you."

"A *cell*. You've broken your promise to me already. I told you how I felt about coming here, to the police station. Are you enjoying this, Inspector?"

"Sorry, enjoying what, Sinty?"

"Toying with my emotions. They are rock bottom, and here you are, adding to my discomfort."

"That's nonsense. All I'm trying to do is carry out my duties as I see fit, and in the process going out of my way to save a young woman's life."

"Who? Whose life?" Sinty demanded.

"That's privileged information. If you'll forgive me, I need to get on. Constable, please make sure Miss Toolah is comfortable in her cell until I can get back to her, hopefully that will be soon."

The female constable stepped forward and tapped Sinty on the shoulder. "If you'd like to come with me, ma'am."

"And if I refuse?" Sinty challenged, her focus boring into Sam.

Sam shrugged. "It makes no odds to me if you want to take your chances out on the streets with a serial killer on the loose."

Sinty groaned and left the room with the constable.

Bob wound up the recording and then asked, "Are you going to tell me what the heck is going on? Whose life is in danger?"

"Marnie Connor, John Wade's niece, has been abducted from school at lunchtime."

"Bugger. Sod it. That's not good news."

"Tell me about it." Sam marched out of the room with her partner close on her heels.

Claire handed Sam the phone number as soon as she entered the incident room.

"I'll make the call from my office, and a coffee wouldn't go amiss, partner."

"Your wish is my command, oh Great One." Bob bowed as she swept past him.

Sam chuckled and closed the door to the office. She paused at the window to take in the view that always tugged on her heartstrings and took a moment to collect her thoughts. Bob came into the room and placed a mug of coffee on her desk then retreated swiftly.

"I'll leave you to it. I don't envy what you're about to go through. I'll be waiting with bated breath."

"Do me a favour. Check in with Liam and Oliver, or chase up Claire, see if she contacted them as I requested. No, wait, that sounds bad, of course she would have done it. See what the outcome was, will you?"

He closed the door behind him, and Sam slipped into her chair and dialled Jessica's number.

"Hello?" the distraught woman replied.

"Hi, Jessica, it's DI Sam Cobbs, returning your call. I'm so sorry to hear the news. Do you have any idea who has taken Marnie?"

"No. I tried to obtain some answers, but the students who saw her go off with the man struggled to give us any more information. You've got to help us, Inspector. My baby, she won't survive. I've gone out of my way to protect her all of her life. She's frail, Marnie was born with a hole in the heart..."

Sobs rippled down the line.

"Jesus, I'm sorry. Please, whatever you do, never lose hope. Do you believe Marnie's abduction is connected to what happened to your brother?"

"Ha, I would have thought that was obvious. Why in God's name do you think I'm ringing you?"

"Sorry, I had to ask. I don't usually believe in coincidences, but maybe there's something else going on in your life that I'm unaware of."

"Such as?"

Sam could sense the woman's anger and tried to calm the situation down before it got out of hand. "Perhaps a split with your partner, something along those lines."

"You couldn't be further from the truth. I have one of the strongest marriages going. Now, tell me, do you have any intention of treating my daughter's abduction seriously or not? Because if you're not willing to, then I demand to know the name of your senior officer, the person you report to on a daily basis. In fact, yes, why don't you do that? Maybe there's a better chance of them finding my daughter alive rather than me be reliant on you."

"I can give you his name by all means, but he has faith in my team's abilities and will only tell us to get on with the case anyway, so the choice is yours."

Jessica growled. "Whatever. We're wasting time arguing the toss about this. My daughter's life is in danger. I'm obviously aware of what this person is capable of, so I'd appreciate less of the small talk and more action on your part, if you don't mind."

"Don't worry, you'll get it. I'll need to know the exact location where your daughter was seen getting into the vehicle and the precise time. That way we can scour the local cameras for any CCTV footage that might be available."

"Grafton Terrace, close to the precinct, do you know it?"

Sam closed her eyes and imagined herself in the area. She glanced around her and then opened her eyes once more. "I do, and yes, I believe there are dozens of cameras in the vicinity."

"Good. Don't let me hold you up any longer. Will you keep me informed?"

"Absolutely, you have my word. We won't let you down. Before you go, how is your brother?"

"Much the same. No improvement as yet, but the doctors aren't surprised, given the extent of his injuries. Please, I don't want my daughter to end up in the hospital, Inspector, or worse, lying in the morgue in one of those damn fridges."

"Trust me, neither do I. I'm going to get on now. I'll be in touch soon."

"Do your best for my daughter."

"I will, I assure you. Take care of yourself, and if the kidnapper gets in touch, please call me right away."

"Wait, the woman I spoke to earlier told me you were

interviewing a suspect, was that to do with my brother's case?"

"Yes. Not exactly a suspect, more a person of interest. I was speaking with the secretary at your brother's firm."

"Ah, I suppose you'd need to do that at some point during the investigation. Did she tell you anything important?"

"Yes and no. At this stage, I can't go into detail. I'll be in touch soon." She ended the call before Jessica had a chance to bombard her with more questions. Time was of the essence. Sam immediately made another call. This time the recipient was Jackie Penrose, the press officer at the station.

"Hello, Jackie, it's me, pest calling."

Jackie's cute laugh echoed down the line. "Hi, Sam. When do you need one?"

"How did you know?"

"Oh, let me guess, the only time you ring me is when you need me to arrange an urgent press conference, am I right?"

"You're spot on. What are the chances? I've got a serial killer causing havoc in the town and now I believe he's kidnapped a teenager. He's already slaughtered three of her relatives, therefore, as you can imagine, I'm considering it a major concern."

"Bloody hell. Let me make some calls and I'll get back to you within ten minutes."

"You're amazing. Thanks, Jackie."

Sam finished her coffee and returned her empty cup to the drinks station but resisted the temptation to refill it.

"Right, gang. Listen up. The first thing we need to do is view the footage at the precinct. Jessica informed me that Marnie went missing in Grafton Terrace. I know that area is significantly covered by cameras, so there's every hope that we will capture the abduction and gain valuable evidence from the footage."

"I can get that arranged, boss," Claire offered.

Sam nodded. "We need to up our pace on this one, we know how dangerous this Nowak is. After hearing what he's been through himself, I can understand his desire to fulfil his need for revenge. And no, that's not me showing any sign of sympathy for him. I've also been on the phone to the press officer. She's doing her utmost to arrange an early press conference. I think it's important to get the news out there promptly. I have to ask, do we have any footage of Nowak that we can use? I'm going to need a clear photo of him for obvious reasons."

"We've got what came in from Cole's neighbour. I could chase that up with the lab, if you like?" Bob said, with his phone in his hand, ready to make the call.

"Do that, thanks, partner. Alex, any news from your angle?"

"Nope, still chasing up a few leads, boss. I sense I'm getting close, if that's any consolation?"

"It is. Stick with it. What about Liam and Oliver, I don't suppose they've been in touch, have they?"

"I called them, all clear at that end. Maybe they'd be better off returning to base."

"I'd rather leave them in situ for now. Let's see if Nowak gets flustered and makes the wrong call."

"You reckon he's going to take the girl back to his flat?" Bob asked.

"We don't know what other properties he has at his disposal, where he might be holding her, do we? If that's his intention. On the other hand, he might choose to just kill her and move on, like he has the others."

"I suppose so," her partner agreed.

Two hours later, Jackie had come up trumps and requested the attendance of members of the press, who were all eager to cover the story. Sam put out the usual plea, inviting the general public to get in touch with the station urgently with any useful information.

Now it was a waiting game, for all of them.

Sam watched the afternoon news go out on TV. She cringed at every slip-up she made during the conference.

Bob observed her reaction. "You did well, considering the pressure you were under to get the information out there."

"Thanks. There were one or two spots where I felt I could have done better."

"You're being too hard on yourself."

The phone rang on Claire's desk. Sam rushed across the room to stand next to the sergeant as she took the call. Sam reached over and hit the speaker button.

"And your name is?" Claire asked.

"Natalia Majewski."

"And you said you know Jakub Nowak well?"

"I do. We good friends. He... oh God, I don't know how to say this without getting him into trouble."

Sam butted into the conversation, "Any information you can give us regarding his whereabouts would be most welcome."

"I... I... I can't... tell you that. But this is so difficult for me."

"Please, you must tell us, a young woman's life is at risk. Hence me putting out an urgent appeal earlier. Tell us what you know, I'm begging you."

Heavy sighing sounded on the other end of the phone. Sam closed her eyes, praying the woman wouldn't feel pressured by her and hang up.

"He took my car. We were visiting a friend last night... I stayed over, and this morning, when I went outside the house, the car, *my* car, it was gone. He must have taken the keys out of my handbag. He didn't mean to do any of this, I'm sure. You don't know what he's been through these last few weeks, months."

"Since the loss of his family?" Sam asked.

Natalia gasped. "You know about that?"

"We know everything there is to know about Jakub, except where to find him. Please, can you help us? You obviously want to do the right thing otherwise you wouldn't have called the station."

"I do, I have to. He needs help. His mind is... how you put it?"

"He's confused? Doesn't know right from wrong?"

"Yes, it's as you say, he confused. His family meant everything to him, and they took them away from him. In our country, people have to pay for the suffering they cause, it's only right that this should happen."

Sam cringed and cautiously continued, aware that if she gave the wrong impression the woman could end the call, and then where would they be? "I understand, Natalia. My heart goes out to him, it must have been torture living with the cruel, endless nightmares of losing his family. That's what's driven him to take his revenge, isn't it?"

"Yes. My friends and I have done what we can to help him, tried to tell him not to take revenge, but it was no use. He told us he killed the family at the beginning of the week. Did he also kill the other family I saw mentioned on the news as well?"

"Yes, at least we're presuming that to be the case. He's now abducted an innocent teenager who is ill. She doesn't deserve to get dragged into this."

"Who is she? You didn't say on the news."

"She's the niece of John Wade, he was the first victim. Please help me save her. He's lost so much this week. Marnie has nothing to do with this. She's an outsider caught up in something that she knows nothing about. Won't you help us find them?"

"How can I do that? I don't know where he is. My boyfriend call round his flat early this morning but he was out, we don't know where else to try."

"Okay, there are ways around this. Can you give us the numberplate of your vehicle? We can run a trace on it through the ANPRs throughout the town."

Natalia gave them the number, and Claire jotted it down. Sam issued a thumbs-up for Claire to begin the search.

"Thanks, I'm sure that will be a huge help. What about places he likes to hang out, or where, as friends, you like to meet up sometimes?"

"Let me think. During the summer we enjoy having picnics down by the river at different spots."

"Okay, what about any buildings he might have access to?"

"No, his flat, but if Ned said he wasn't there then there is little point in you going over there to find him."

"No, we tried that earlier and drew a blank. Do you think he's likely to remain in the area, or is there a possibility that he might move on?"

"I don't know. His state of mind is in question to me, does that make sense?" she queried, doubting her English.

"Perfectly. Your English is very good. Have you lived here long?"

"Yes, around five years. I have had far more opportunities to get work in this country. I love Poland, but it is being ruined by our government. My people spend most of their time rebelling against the useless government."

"I can imagine. I'm glad you feel safe here. Did you travel here illegally?"

"No, I have papers. I work here legally and pay my taxes

like every good Polish citizen I know. Even Jakub, he pay taxes, too."

"Where does he work?"

"In a factory on the other side of Workington. Not sure what it's called. They make plastic, no idea what for."

"Brilliant, that's something we can check up. Is there anything else? What about his friends, does anyone have use of a building that isn't frequently used?"

"Gosh, I don't know. I will have to think about this. Can I call you back?"

"Of course you can, you have our number. Don't be afraid to use it if anything else comes to mind. Can you ask around your friends? Maybe someone else will be able to think of somewhere. It's important, if we're going to save this young lady."

"Okay. I do this for you, and for Jakub, he needs to be caught, he's a danger to himself and other people now. I've kept quiet for long enough about this."

Something occurred to Sam, and she felt obliged to ask Natalia, "Is it possible that he might leave the country and go back to Poland?"

"I don't think so. Umm, wait, there was talk about him going to France a few weeks ago. Our friends urged him to get away for a while."

"Would your car be up for the trip?"

"I don't understand what you're asking."

"Is your car in perfect condition, good enough to be used for a long-distance trip like travelling to France?"

"Oh, yes, yes, I get what you mean now. Yes, it's serviced regularly, in perfect nick as my boyfriend likes to say."

"Okay, that's another route open to us. Thank you so much for getting in touch. Don't forget to ask around your friends, see if they can come up with somewhere he's likely to be holding the teenager."

"I'll do that now and get back to you. I hope he does the right thing and let her go before he causes her any harm. He's not a bad person, not deep down. But losing his family has destroyed him. You have to put yourself in his shoes."

"I completely get that, I really do, but this young lady is an innocent bystander who doesn't deserve to die, if that's his intention."

"I wouldn't know, I hope not."

"Goodbye, Natalia. Hopefully speak soon."

"Yes. Okay, goodbye."

Claire hung up, and Sam perched on the desk behind her, exhausted by the call and her desire not to screw it up.

"Let's hope she comes back to us with a possible location. Claire, can you issue an alert for the car while we go over the footage? I sense we're getting closer, but if he's already hinted at leaving the country, how the hell are we going to stop him?"

Bob left his seat and approached Sam. "We need to warn all the ports in the area. Scrap that, he could be miles away by now. What...? Don't look at me like that. He could be, if he's got the use of a reliable car and is on the run. I'd head as far south as I could and jump on a ferry or even get on board the Eurotunnel."

"Well, you'd better alert all the relevant authorities then and issue an alert that will cover the whole of the UK, that includes Ireland and the Isle of Man, which is within spitting distance of us."

Bob paused mid-step. "Now there's a thought."

"What?" Sam queried.

"What if he's hopped aboard a boat, or stolen one and crossed over to the Isle of Man? It's doable."

Sam nodded. It gained momentum the more she considered his idea. "Get in touch with the police over there. Ask them to do the necessary checks at the ports on the island.

I've never been there so I don't know how many ports it has."

"On it now." Bob rushed back to his desk.

Sam's head whirled. "Would he risk going out of the country? What about the girl's passport? Border control are shit-hot these days since we've come out of Brexit. I don't want to waste all of our effort only to draw a blank."

The team got to work. Alex located the plastics firm. Sam rang the number and spoke to the person in charge, who advised her to speak to the line manager who told her that Jakub hadn't shown up for work all week, he rang in sick on Monday.

Great. That much was obvious and no help to their investigation at all.

It wasn't until late afternoon, when Sam had recalled Oliver and Liam to the station, that things looked promising. An officer out on patrol had called in to say he'd spotted the car leaving the town around lunchtime. It had drawn his attention because the male driver was weaving in and out of the traffic, but the constable was on another call and didn't have time to pull the car over.

"Shit! Could this be an opportunity missed?" Sam mumbled.

"It's wrong of you to think negatively," Bob reprimanded her gently. "It's a significant lead, more than we had earlier."

"I just wish Natalia would call in. We need her more than ever now."

"She will, I'm sure of it. Let me get you a coffee."

Sam shook her head. "I'm full to the brim, in fact, I need to spend a penny, thanks for the reminder."

She headed off down the corridor and returned to Claire frantically waving to gain her attention.

She covered the mouthpiece of the phone. "It's Natalia, she only wants to speak to you."

Sam hit the speaker button. "Natalia, thank you so much for getting back to me. Have you got a possible location for us?"

"I spoke to all of Jakub's friends. They're as devastated as me, but we all want to help save this girl. Enough people have died this week, we want to prevent him from taking her life as well."

"Thank you, it means a lot, knowing that you all feel the same way and are willing to work with us."

"Good. I hope you won't forget it and you will show some compassion towards Jakub if you find him."

"You have my word, he will be treated with the utmost respect. Where is the location?"

"He's often spoken about working on a farm, having lots of rescue animals, sheep, cows, pigs that farmers prefer to send to the slaughterhouse. He told us this one day when we were out on a lovely walk in the countryside. Not long after, we stumbled across an old barn that had seen better days."

Sam crossed her fingers as the team gathered around her to listen to the conversation.

"Can you remember where it was?"

"Between us, we came up with this location. It's a village called Ullock. It has the river running close by. We walked along by the river and saw the barn. Jakub was keen to investigate it, and a couple of the men went off to have a nose around while the women set up the picnic for lunch. Jakub came back all excited and revealed big plans of one day owning the barn for when his family arrived."

Sam watched Claire bring up a map of the area on her screen and zoom in on the properties in the village. Oliver pointed at the bottom, to an old barn which was situated close to the river.

"I think we've found it on the map. Leave it with us, we'll

see what we can find. I can't thank you enough for this. Will you pass on my thanks to your friends?"

"I will. Please, you promised me you would respect Jakub."

"I always keep my promises. Take care." Sam ended the call. "We need to get the helicopter out there to have a look around. Tell them not to make it obvious. If they can spot the car at the location, then that's our job done."

Bob actioned the request and reported back to Sam. "They're en route now. I told them that we wouldn't be far behind them."

"Good call. We should all get on the road. It's what? About fifteen to twenty minutes from here?"

"Depends on the traffic. It's getting late, we're likely to get held up in the rush-hour traffic."

Sam kicked out at the chair standing next to her. "Not what I want to hear. Okay, let's all set off anyway. Claire, you and Suzanna stay here and monitor our progress. Contact us if you hear anything. The rest of you, come with me. We'll take two cars."

CHAPTER 10

Bob was in regular contact with the police helicopter, and Sam used the siren to piss off the public during the busiest hour of the day. Workington was often a nightmare to navigate, even the shortcuts dotted around the town were chocka nine-tenths of the time.

"This is driving me sodding nuts. Get out of my way, bloody morons."

"Calm down, you'll give yourself a heart attack," Bob chirped from the passenger seat, pissing Sam off even more.

She was about to retaliate with a tirade of abuse, but he silenced her with his hand when the pilot of the chopper got in touch.

"Go ahead," Bob shouted.

"I'm coming up to the barn now, and yes, there's a dark Peugeot 405 outside it. Can't actually view the numberplate as yet."

"Tell them not to make it obvious," Sam reiterated.

Bob passed on the message.

"Don't worry, a quick fly over from a distance and you'll

have your answer. I'll land in one of the nearby fields, hang around on standby, in case you need me."

"Roger that," Bob replied.

Sam swallowed down the bile burning her throat. "This is it. Are you ready to save the day, big man?"

Bob turned to face her and smirked. "Ready, willing and exceptionally able. Are you?"

"I signed a Taser out, so yes, all ready. Let's hope we're not too late and he hasn't harmed the girl yet."

"I've got a feeling that's wishful thinking on your part."

"Crap, don't say that. I bet she's terrified. If she survives this situation, it'll probably scar her emotionally for life."

"No point getting yourself worked up about it, we can deal with the consequences after the danger has been eliminated."

"True enough. Can you contact the others? Make them aware of the situation and tell them to be prepared to hit the ground running once we arrive. I don't think we should hang around."

"What? You're going to hit him hard and fast? Are you sure about that?"

"Don't put doubts in my mind, not at this late stage."

Bob slammed his head against the headrest. "I'm not, not intentionally. It's the opposite to how you usually tackle this type of scenario. Why the change?"

"I suppose because of the aggressive nature of the murders so far. I think if he gets wind that we're around, he's going to pounce on the girl and won't think twice about slicing her throat, like he did with the other kids."

"I think I prefer it when you're contemplative in the car and in a world of your own. That way, I don't have to deal with all these dark images you evoke."

Sam laughed. "You're an idiot of massive proportions."

"Correct, and you'd be utterly mortified if I wasn't the adorable cheeky chappie you know and love."

"Steady on now, nothing like building your part."

The rest of the journey was completed in relative silence with Bob instructing her to take a right or left every now and again. The closer Sam got to Ullock, the more the large, twisted knot constricted her stomach.

Come on, girl, I've got this. I've brought down worse criminals than this in the past. Have I? I have my doubts whether that is true or not. We'll soon find out.

"Over the brow of the next hill, according to the map." Proving his point, Bob flashed her the Google Map on his phone.

"Right, so this is probably the entrance coming up on the right." Sam indicated and braked to make the rest of the team following aware.

The barn was directly in front of them, the stolen car parked up outside the entrance to it. Sam drew to a halt and lowered the window. All was quiet until a girl's scream erupted inside the barn.

"That's it. I'm not hanging around, it's now or never." Sam wrenched open the door and left it swaying in the slight breeze.

Bob did the same, and they both ran towards the opening of the huge wooden-slatted building. With her back against the side of the barn, Sam glanced back to see Oliver, Liam and Alex jump out of the car and run towards them, using the patch of grass to deaden their footsteps.

"We're going to head in there, we heard the girl scream and nothing since. Let's hope we're not too late."

"Why don't we keep one person out here? They can add an element of surprise if things become hairy in there," Bob suggested.

"I'm up for that. I can remain in the doorway, cut off the exit," Liam said, Taser in hand.

"Makes sense. Okay, first sign of him running off, take him down, Liam, got that?"

"Yes, boss."

"On the count of three, we walk in there. Be prepared to react if the girl is in trouble." It was the best Sam could come up with without knowing first-hand how dangerous the situation was inside the barn. "Ready?"

The others raised their thumbs, each of them looking as nervous as she was.

Get over it. Marnie needs me to be on top of my game and rescue her.

Sam was the first to move. She rounded the corner and gasped when she saw a young blonde girl standing petrified amongst the bales of straw, a tightened noose around her neck. Holding the other end of the rope was the man who Sam presumed to be Jakub.

Shit, shit, shit!

Taser drawn and pointed at Jakub's chest, Sam introduced herself. "Now, Jakub, don't do anything rash here. I'm DI Sam Cobbs. Why don't you drop the rope and we'll discuss this?" Her gaze drifted to the wide-eyed girl who was crying, probably relieved that she'd been discovered.

But she wasn't out of the woods yet, not by a long shot.

"You won't save her, I won't allow it." He took up the slack in the rope which he'd thrown over a beam directly above Marnie.

The girl sobbed and whispered, "Please don't do this. I haven't done anything wrong. I don't want to die."

"Neither did they," Jakub said through gritted teeth.

"I know what happened to your family, Jakub. Believe me, we're all truly sorry for your loss, but this isn't going to help,"

Sam said. "Don't you think you've shed enough blood this week, killing the others?"

Jakub stared at her, his gaze travelling the length of her body before returning to her face. "What do you know?"

"I know two wrongs don't make a right. We all agree the loss of your family must have been excruciating for you, but you're going about this all the wrong way. You should have trusted the police, confided in us when you lost your family. We would have been eager to help you bring Wade and Thompson to justice. How has killing their families eased your pain?"

After a lengthy pause, the rope slackened a little, and he said, "Intentionally leaving them alive, to suffer, was all part of my plan. Once they got out of hospital, they'd need to contend with their injuries, sit in their homes, alone, with the memories of seeing their wives and children slaughtered. It's impossible to not be affected by that. I live with the images of my family drowning, on that godforsaken boat, every day of my life. Deal with the distressing nightmares. I have to live with the reminder that my family died *because of me*."

"No, they didn't. It was an unfortunate accident, Jakub, no one was to blame, certainly not you."

"I wanted all of this. I saw this place months ago, told my wife about the dreams I had of running it, and she fell in love with the idea. My kids were all excited, too, they'd even chosen names for a few of the animals I wanted to rescue. Our lives were about to change forever until... tragedy took them from me... robbed me of their beautiful smiles. Why? Because the boat wasn't an adequate vessel to make the trip across the sea from France. Who else was to blame for that, if not Wade and Thompson?"

"Please, let us deal with them, this isn't the right way to go about things. Marnie is innocent, she had nothing to do with what happened to your family. Please, please, won't you reconsider?"

The rope grew taut once more. "But she is Wade's family. He doesn't deserve to have any left, not after taking mine from me. I want him to suffer, and this is the only way I know how."

"Marnie rarely sees her uncle anyway," Sam lied, "her mother fell out with her brother a while back, so the only people you'll be hurting, apart from Marnie, is her mother and father. Do you really want them to live with the pain that you're going through, even though they had nothing whatsoever to do with this? Is that fair?"

"Life isn't fair, it never is, is it, Inspector?"

"Yes, it can be. But you're going to need to trust me."

"Why should I trust you? The police don't give a shit about the immigrants, that much is obvious. You take your frustrations out on the people who have been brought into this country illegally and yet you allow the bastards who dangled the golden carrot to bring them here to go unpunished."

Sam shook her head. "Sometimes that must seem how it is, but I assure you, nothing could be further from the truth. We're clamping down on people like Wade and Thompson, but most of the time they operate under our radar, and we're reliant on the information we obtain from people like you, so that we can bring them to justice."

"You need to be more aware of these smugglers and the desperate individuals they put in danger. People travel the wild seas to achieve a more fulfilling life."

"How is that our fault? We're an island that is tiny in comparison to other countries such as France, Germany and Spain, and yet people always want to come here. Why? Because they know they'll be looked after well. That's not always the case, as you've found out. People like Wade and

Thompson have contacts in the underworld, the dross of our community. Their involvement is all about greed and lining their own pockets. If people are desperate to come to this country, they need to take the appropriate measures and apply for a visa to live and work here. None of this is our fault. I suppose what I'm trying to say is, why punish Marnie for her uncle's imperfections?"

Marnie whimpered and was forced to stand on her tiptoes as Jakub wrapped the rope around his wrists. The line went rigid, and Sam feared he was about to give it a final tug soon. She had to think of another way to get through to him, to highlight the error of his ways.

Out of the corner of her eye, Sam caught Liam raise his Taser. He'd have the perfect shot from where he was standing, if things came to a head. But Sam was determined for it not to come to that.

"Jakub, let the girl go and come back to the station with me. I'll take a formal statement from you about what happened to your family, and we'll work together, make sure we throw everything we've got at Wade and Thompson. I have no intention of allowing either of them to get away with this."

"Talk, it's all talk. You should have dealt with them before."

Sam nodded. "I'm not denying that. If we'd been aware of what they were up to, then yes, we would have arrested them."

"It's rife, this disgusting trade. You cops need to open your eyes, take note of what's going on around you. Instead, you let innocent people, like my wife and children, suffer the consequences. How is that right?"

He wound the rope an extra loop around his wrist. Marnie's eyes widened, and she teetered on the tips of her toes.

Sam's heart lurched at the girl's plight. "Please, let's talk about this before you do anything rash that you're likely to regret."

"I have no regrets, not when it comes to punishing their families. She's going to die, just like the others. Meet the worst possible end of her life, just like my family did. It was all my idea to come and settle in England. My wife remained in Poland, reluctant to come here. It wasn't until our little one became sick and we were unable to receive the treatment he needed back in Poland that she begged me to let her and my children come, to consider making the horrendous trip that ended their lives. I was so excited, tried to make plans for our future… only for it all to end when that boat went down. Now, I can't bear it when I wake up every day. I pray every night for God to take me, but He keeps me on this earth, to be punished. How is that right? I'm trying to give my life back to Him, but He refuses to take it. Why? To cause me yet more pain? Or is His intention to keep me here so I can avenge their deaths?"

"I'm sorry, I can't answer that. What I do know is that He wouldn't want you to take yet another innocent life in this way. Let her go, Jakub. Trust me, we'll get you the justice you and your family deserve, through the courts."

"Ha, that's a laugh. Since coming here I've been appalled at how lenient your courts are. It's laughable, the sentences the judges over here hand out to people like Wade and Thompson. What kind of message is that sending out to people who are willing to take advantage of others for money?"

He had a point, she couldn't deny that. "Sentencing is out of my hands, but I can still do my part for your family. Please, give me the chance to do that."

"Why should I? I know how you cops like to gain someone's trust only to arrest them. I won't allow that to happen. I have a job I need to carry out, and neither you nor your goons are going to stop me."

With that, his legs straightened, and he leaned backwards. Marnie's slender body was hoisted up into the air.

"No," Sam shouted. She fired her Taser at Jakub, but he turned to the side and she missed. "Liam, do it."

Her trusted Taser partner left his post and fired, making a direct hit. Bob, Alex and Oliver all ran forward to catch Marnie as her body hurtled to the ground. Sam jumped into action and relieved Jakub of the rope. She let out a sigh and ordered Liam to remove the wires from the man's chest while she stood by and waited to slap her cuffs on him.

"How is she?" Sam called over, once everything settled down.

"She seems fine, but I think we should call an ambulance to be on the safe side," Bob shouted.

"Do it. I'll ring her mother, let her know she's been rescued. Liam, put Jakub in the car. Oliver, can you help him? I don't want any slip-ups now that we've come this far."

Jakub sat up, dazed. "I want to die, kill me."

"We don't do things like that in this country, Jakub. You'll go to prison and you'll probably end up in the cell next to Wade and Thompson."

"Good, I'll finish them off inside," he sneered.

Sam hitched up a shoulder. "Whatever. As long as you all get what you deserve, I couldn't care less what happens next."

"See, you pretend you care when you don't."

"Oh, I care all right. It's my job to keep the public safe, and that's what my team and I have successfully achieved today."

"Bullshit. You don't give a toss, no one in authority in this country gives a damn. Why do you think the crime rate is at an all-time high? We prefer to take the law into our own hands."

"Then that makes you no better than Wade or Thompson in my opinion. Get him out of here."

Oliver and Liam pulled Jakub to his feet. He tried to kick out and put up a fight, but Sam's colleagues coped admirably with restraining him. She watched them drag him to their car and place him in the back seat. She removed her mobile from her pocket and dialled a number.

"Yes, who is this?"

"Jessica, it's DI Sam Cobbs. Are you sitting down?"

"Oh God, is she dead? Please, don't let her be dead."

Sam handed the phone to Marnie and whispered, "It's your Mum."

"Mummy... I'm safe, they saved me." Poor Marnie broke down in tears and passed the phone back to Sam.

Jessica was also overwhelmed on the other end.

"Come on, now," Sam said. "I told you we'd save her. Dry your tears, Jessica."

"Thank you, thank you. You don't know what this means to me, she's my world, my everything."

"I can imagine. We've called an ambulance to attend the scene, just as a precaution. I won't have any further news for you until it arrives. Can you bear with me, and I'll get back to you soon?"

"Yes, you do what you have to do. An ambulance, is she injured?"

Sam ran a hand down Marnie's red neck where the rope had scratched her. "She looks fine to me, but it'll be better if we get her checked out. You wouldn't forgive me if we neglected to do that, would you?"

"No, I suppose not. Thank you again. I'll have my phone with me at all times."

"Take care."

Sam ended the call and patted Bob and Alex on the back. "We did good, boys."

"We saved the day again," Bob added.

THE AMBULANCE ARRIVED twenty-five minutes later. By then, Marnie was feeling a lot better. Grateful and appreciative that she had survived her ordeal. She refused to go to hospital. The paramedics checked her over and were happy to release her to go home.

Sam thanked them for attending so promptly. The four of them got in the car. Sam sat in the back, holding hands with Marnie. Bob drove, and Alex accompanied them in the passenger seat.

Marnie flew into her mother's arms as soon as they drew up outside the family home. Sam stood back and allowed the mother and daughter their long-awaited reunion. Jessica released her hold on her daughter and opened her arms to give Sam a hug. Sam stepped towards her with tears in her eyes.

"I'm glad we were able to save her, it doesn't always turn out that way."

Jessica released her and said, "I'm so thankful we had you working on the investigation. It might have concluded very differently if we hadn't."

Sam smiled. "You're going to hate me for what I'm about to say next."

Jessica inclined her head and asked, "What's that?"

"We've discovered that your brother and his partner were operating a people-trafficking operation via their business."

"What? Is that what this has been all about?"

"Yes, Jakub Nowak, the man who kidnapped Marnie, was out for revenge."

"Revenge? I don't understand."

"His family perished, along with others, in a boat bound for England off the coast of the Isle of Wight."

TO HOLD RESPONSIBLE

"No. He must have been inconsolable. But that didn't give him the right to kill my sister-in-law and my nephew and nieces or put Marnie through this ordeal. Please don't tell me you're going to go easy on him."

Sam shook her head. "No way. I'll tell you what I told him: two wrongs don't make a right."

"Exactly. I won't tell the rest of my family. If you say my brother is guilty, then that's good enough for me. He was wrong and needs to be punished. Shame on him for putting his family at risk, for putting us all at risk."

"I wanted you to know. I felt you deserved to know the truth."

"Thank you. I appreciate it, Inspector."

THEY DROVE BACK to the station. Within ten minutes of their arrival, Sam and Bob were sitting in an interview room, questioning Jakub Nowak. It made a pleasant change for the suspect not to go down the 'no comment' route. Instead, Jakub insisted on telling them everything, although he showed little remorse for any of the horrendous crimes he had committed from kidnapping, Grievous Bodily Harm to murder. If anything, his defiance was the main reason the tiny amount of sympathy Sam had for him went out of the window. After she'd heard enough, Sam instructed her partner, along with the constable who had joined them during the interview, to escort Jakub to his cell.

Wearily, Sam ascended the stairs and returned to her office, where she rang Rhys to let him know how her day had panned out and also to inform him that she would be home at her usual time. "How's Casper been today?" she asked.

"He's been amazing. I've given him lots of walks. Don't laugh, but instead of typing up my notes at the end of every consultation, I've invested in a Dictaphone. I use it to take down my notes while I'm out with Casper, then my secretary types them up when I get back. That frees up a little spare time to do some extra training with Casper at the park."

"I knew you would find a solution sooner rather than later. He's a good boy, Rhys. He's never going to replace Benji, but I have no doubt he'll come a close second to him."

"You're always right, I should realise that by now. What do you fancy for dinner tonight?"

"Nothing much. I think there's a chilli in the freezer, that with rice will do me."

"Sounds good enough for me. See you later, and congratulations on cracking yet another case."

She ended the call, leaned her head back and closed her eyes for a moment or two. Bob found her in the same position ten minutes later. She had dozed off, something she never did. It just went to show how much days living on her nerves had taken out of her.

"We're going for a swift one at the pub. Do you want to join us? Hey, you weren't asleep, were you?"

Straightening the kinks out of her back and rotating her shoulders, she replied, "Don't be so ridiculous, I was resting my eyes, that's all."

"There you go again, trying to kid a kidder."

"Whatever. I'm still going to take a rain check, if that's okay? How was Jakub when you left him?"

He took a seat. "He seemed depressed. At least he had the decency to give us the lowdown on all the crimes he'd committed. You know how that usually turns out if the suspect is reluctant to open up to us."

Sam stretched her arms above her head and nodded. "Only too well. Thank God we saved Marnie. If we hadn't shown up when we did… well, it doesn't bear thinking about."

"Now all we have to do is arrest the other two fuckers, Wade and Thompson."

Her mood deflated rapidly. "Yeah, that isn't going to be easy."

Bob wagged a finger. "You can pack that in. There's no way you should show any damn sympathy towards those morons, Sam."

"I'm not, believe me. However, my heart goes out to their families, or those left behind. How are they going to feel once they hear the bloody truth?"

Bob's chin dipped onto his chest. "Yeah, I suppose I never thought about that side of things. What a frigging mess! And the secretary?"

"She'll be charged as an accessory. She had knowledge of what was going on and did nothing to prevent it. In my opinion, that makes her as culpable as Wade and Thompson."

Bob's head rose, and their gazes met. "That's going to go down like a mouldy jam sandwich at a chimps' tea party."

Her nose wrinkled. "Seriously? Where the heck did that one come from?"

Before he could respond, Sam's mobile rang. She glanced at the caller ID and saw her sister's name on the screen. "Hang on, it's Crystal."

He stood. "No, I'll give you some privacy."

"Thanks, matey. Hey, Crystal, this is a pleasant surprise. I was going to give you a call tonight. What's up?"

"Hi, I've got some bad news."

Sam sat upright and swept the hair away from her ear. "I'm listening. Are you okay?"

"I am, it's Mum. She's in hospital."

EPILOGUE

Sam tore through the incident room and bounded down the stairs two at a time.

"Sam, is everything okay? Sam?" Bob shouted from the top of the stairs.

Ignoring him, she left the station and jumped into her car. She was aware of the regulations about using the siren when on personal business, but to hell with that. Her mother's life was in danger.

She gripped the steering wheel tightly, the skin on her knuckles stretching until it was paper thin. All she could think about was her mother lying on an operating table.

"Rhys, it's me. You're going to have to listen carefully to me."

"Sam, you're worrying me, what's going on? Are you all right? What's with the siren?"

"No, I'm on my way to Whitehaven Hospital."

"What? Why? Are you hurt? Are you in an ambulance? Tell me, for God's sake!"

"No, it's nothing like that. I'm fine, it's Mum. Apparently, she was involved in a three-car pile-up and is on her way to the operating theatre. Crystal just rang me, summoned me to the hospital to be with her and Dad."

"Damn, do you want me to join you?"

She sensed the panic rising within him. "No, let me get there and see how the land lies first. You stay with the boys. I'll call you back, if and when I have some more news."

"Okay, if you're sure. Drive carefully. I love you. And try not to worry too much, she's in safe hands."

"Thanks, I'm doing my best. Love you, too."

Sam conducted the rest of the journey on autopilot. She pulled up outside A&E. After parking the car illegally, she ran through the entrance and announced who she was at the desk. The receptionist, who Sam had dealt with before, smiled and said hello.

"I'm sorry, this is an emergency. My mother has been brought in after being involved in a pile-up. Her name is Jill Lucas. Can you tell me how I can get to her, or at least be with the rest of my family? My sister called me about fifteen minutes ago. I think Mum was on her way down to surgery. Damn, I'm not thinking straight, please, you have to help me."

"Okay, take a breath. You've given me all the information I need to search the system." The receptionist fell silent, and her fingers danced across the keyboard. "Right, I've got her. Yes, she's due to have an operation within the next few minutes."

"How do I get there?"

"Take a left out of the building and follow the road round until you get to the parking area on the right. Go through to the entrance and ask a member of staff there, they'll be of further assistance to you. Are you okay to drive?"

"Yes. Thanks so much for all your help."

"Hope your mother is going to be okay."

Sam smiled and bolted back out to the car. She hadn't

driven far when she noticed her brother-in-law, Vernon, standing outside the hospital entrance. She parked the car and slapped her usual notice on the dashboard, alerting the parking attendants that she was on official business, even though she wasn't.

She ran across the road. Vernon appeared to be in a world of his own and didn't see her.

"Hey, Vernon. How is she, do you know?"

His eyes bulged. "I'm sorry, Sam. I don't want to be the one to tell you, it's not my place. Come inside, your father and Crystal are waiting for you."

She grasped his arm, her legs buckling beneath her. "Oh God. She's not... dead, is she?"

He stared at her, his expression blank. Overwhelmed, Sam collapsed.

THE END

Thank you for reading To Hold Responsible the next thrilling adventure **To Catch a Killer**

Have you read any of my fast paced other crime thrillers yet? Why not try the first book in the DI Sara Ramsey series No Right to Kill

Or grab the first book in the bestselling, award-winning, Justice series here, Cruel Justice.

Or the first book in the spin-off Justice Again series, Gone In Seconds.

. . .

PERHAPS YOU'D PREFER to try one of my other police procedural series, the DI Kayli Bright series which begins with The Missing Children.

OR MAYBE YOU'D enjoy the DI Sally Parker series set in Norfolk, Wrong Place.

OR MY GRITTY police procedural starring DI Nelson set in Manchester, Torn Apart.

OR MAYBE YOU'D like to try one of my successful psychological thrillers She's Gone, I KNOW THE TRUTH or Shattered Lives.

TO KEEP IN TOUCH WITH M A COMLEY

Pick up a FREE novella by signing up to my newsletter today.
https://BookHip.com/WBRTGW

BookBub
www.bookbub.com/authors/m-a-comley

Blog

http://melcomley.blogspot.com

Why not join my special Facebook group to take part in monthly giveaways.

Readers' Group

Printed in Great Britain
by Amazon